One More to Die

ALSO BY JOY ELLIS

ELLIE MCEWAN SERIES
Book 1: An Aura of Mystery
Book 2: The Colour of Mystery

NOVELLAS
Guard Her With Your Life
One More to Die

JACKMAN & EVANS SERIES
Book 1: The Murderer's Son
Book 2: Their Lost Daughter
Book 3: The Fourth Friend
Book 4: The Guilty Ones
Book 5: The Stolen Boys
Book 6: The Patient Man
Book 7: They Disappeared
Book 8: The Night Thief
Book 9: Solace House
Book 10: The River's Edge

THE NIKKI GALENA SERIES
Book 1: Crime on the Fens
Book 2: Shadow over the Fens
Book 3: Hunted on the Fens
Book 4: Killer on the Fens
Book 5: Stalker on the Fens
Book 6: Captive on the Fens
Book 7: Buried on the Fens
Book 8: Thieves on the Fens
Book 9: Fire on the Fens
Book 10: Darkness on the Fens
Book 11: Hidden on the Fens
Book 12: Secrets on the Fens
Book 13: Fear on the Fens
Book 14: Graves on the Fens
Book 15: Echoes on the Fens

DETECTIVE MATT BALLARD
Book 1: Beware the Past
Book 2: Five Bloody Hearts
Book 3: The Dying Light
Book 4: Marshlight
Book 5: Trick of the Night
Book 6: The Bag of Secrets

ONE MORE TO DIE

JOY ELLIS

JOFFE BOOKS

Joffe Books, London
www.joffebooks.com

First published in Great Britain in 2025

© Joy Ellis

This book is a work of fiction. Names, characters, businesses, organizations, places and events are either the product of the author's imagination or are used fictitiously. Any resemblance to actual persons, living or dead, events or locales is entirely coincidental. The spelling used is British English except where fidelity to the author's rendering of accent or dialect supersedes this. The right of Joy Ellis to be identified as author of this work has been asserted in accordance with the Copyright, Designs and Patents Act 1988.

No part of this book may be used or reproduced in any manner for the purpose of training artificial intelligence technologies or systems. In accordance with Article 4(3) of the Digital Single Market Directive 2019/790, Joffe Books expressly reserves this work from the text and data mining exception.

Cover art by Nick Castle
Cover image by Luke Squelch

ISBN: 978-1-80573-155-9

For our friends, Linda and Rob . . . and Dash!

Wishing you exciting times ahead in your beloved Northumberland. We are going to miss you.

Oh, and a little reminder that you never say anything either intriguing or interesting to a crime writer, Linda, as it might finish up in print! Thank you!

Joy, Jacquie, and the Magnificent Seven xxx

PROLOGUE

Sunday morning, and the house was in uproar. But then it always was. Chaos seemed to be the norm for the Carter family.

'Mum! I can't find my dinosaur T-shirt!'

'In the wash. You put it on Rodders, remember? Then he rolled in the mud.' Kate looked fondly at the long-suffering Labrador, who this morning was only adorned with a bandana declaring him to be better than a Squishmallow. She fondled his ears and decided she couldn't argue with that. 'Now, you lot. Breakfast! Everyone to the table, please.'

As the children took their seats, Tom Carter hurried in from the garden and washed his hands before joining them. 'Remind me to order some more mealworms for Matilda, babe. I've never known a duck eat so much.'

'I've got to order cat and dog food too, so we'll get everything delivered together. The animals eat more than the kids.' What did she expect, with three dogs, two cats, a duck and Brian the tortoise — though at least Brian was cheap to

1

feed. Dandelions and edible weeds were plentiful in their less than manicured garden.

Halfway through breakfast, Kate's mobile rang, and the kitchen fell silent.

She spoke for a few moments, then ended the call. She looked around. 'Sorry, guys, it's work.'

'Action stations! Dive, dive, dive!' yelled Eddie, holding his nose. He then slid off his chair and disappeared under the table.

'Get Carter!' squealed seven-year-old Chloe. She had no idea where the saying came from, but she'd heard her dad repeat it, so that was fine by her.

Timmy, the youngest, rolled his eyes, but said nothing. He was always more attentive to his food than the others, and was relieved that the call had come after his breakfast had been served.

'Sorry, sweetheart,' Kate said to Tom. 'Still, we got two days together, that's pretty good compared to usual.'

'Almost a record.' Tom grinned at her. 'Go and do your thing, babe; we've got it covered here, haven't we, kids?'

Kate grabbed a piece of toast and ran upstairs to change.

Eight minutes later, with her long fair hair now swept into an elegant chignon and her PJ bottoms discarded, Detective Inspector Kate Carter of the Serious Crimes Unit, now dressed in a smart navy suit, stepped out of the house.

Her Kia Sportage was parked close to the front gates, positioned for a swift exit. She pressed her key to unlock it, but before she climbed in, she saw something under her windscreen wiper.

She cursed, wishing people wouldn't stick advertising fliers on cars, then saw it was an envelope with *Kate* written on it.

She frowned and ripped it open, took out the single sheet of white paper, and read:

You are the most beautiful woman I've ever seen.

The frown deepened, and Kate muttered, 'Yeah, right. And you are an arsehole.' She balled up the paper and dropped it onto the drive. Right now, she had a suspicious death to attend to, and that took precedence over some creep who needed stronger glasses.

***

A few minutes after her car had rounded the corner at the end of the road, a figure stepped from the shelter of the trees that edged the Carter garden. He knelt down and picked up the screwed-up paper.

As he walked away, he held it up to his face and inhaled deeply. He smiled. Was there just the slightest hint of her perfume on it? He thought there was. He took a long, shuddery breath, put it carefully in his pocket and walked on.

CHAPTER ONE

Detective Inspector Kate Carter stood close to the edge of the deep ditch and stared down at the wreckage.

'I'm guessing I wouldn't have been dragged from the bosom of my adoring family if this was just some drunken prat who overcooked that sharp bend on the fen lane?'

'My words exactly,' said DS Geraldine Wilde, her detective sergeant. 'Although my family aren't quite as adoring as yours.'

Kate knew that to be true. Gerry and her son, Nathan, were temporarily back with her parents following an acrimonious split with her husband. She got on well with her father, who idolised her son, but her mother was a difficult woman who had honed criticism of others, especially Gerry, into a fine art. Kate hoped, for Gerry's sake, that her stay would not be a long one.

'Uniform took one look at the car and its occupant, then had what PC "Chick" Fowler called the screaming ab-dabs, and shouted for CID,' said Gerry, staring down into the ditch. 'Nothing adds up. The number plate's a fake; the windscreen

ID number has been etched out; the engine number has been obliterated; the man has a photo ID driving licence on him that clearly isn't his, and — what else? Oh, Chick didn't like the fact that one of the tyres doesn't match the other three.'

'And other than that, everything is hunky dory,' muttered Kate.

'Did I forget to mention that the driver's been stabbed?' Gerry gave her an innocent smile. 'Beneath all that blood from when he hit the windscreen, there's a neat little puncture wound in his neck from a thin-bladed knife.'

'Ah, yet another mystery for lucky old SCU to unscramble.' Kate was now looking at the accident site with fresh eyes. 'Are the SOCOs on their way? I assume forensics have been called?'

'Oh yes, they should be here any minute, and uniform have a team on the way to cordon this off. They've already closed entry at both ends of the lane. It's only a cut-through that avoids the A-road, and it's mainly used by farm vehicles. Chick told me they've already notified the farmer whose land this is, and he'll make alternative arrangements to access his fields.'

'Good.' Kate looked at the nondescript vehicle. It was an old Ford Focus, and not all the dents on it were down to taking a head dive into a ditch. A disposable vehicle, perfect for driving into a ditch with an already dead body in it. 'Gerry? Got any of your famous intuitions about this one?'

Gerry shrugged. 'Not yet — unless you count knowing damn well that this could be the tip of an iceberg.' She jabbed a finger at the rear off-side wheel. 'And if old Chick's copper's nose is correct, I'll be very interested to know about that.'

Kate nodded. It was an expensive Continental tyre, and by the look of them, the others were remoulds. That sort of anomaly stood out like a sore thumb to the older bobbies, who could spot a dodgy motor a mile off. 'Normally, I'd say that there'll be something concealed inside,' she said. 'But not in this case. Surely whoever topped our dead guy would have taken the drugs, or whatever was stashed there, before they used the car as a coffin?'

Gerry puffed out her cheeks. 'What if they didn't notice? It would have been dark when this car went into the ditch. Maybe it did belong to the driver. He could have been killed and bundled back into his own motor, and our killer, or killers, didn't see that odd tyre.'

'Possible, I suppose, but we need to know a whole lot more before we start trying to piece this together.' Kate looked up as a white van bearing the words "Crime Scene Investigation" approached. 'Here's the SOCOs, and it looks like we're graced by the presence of Cold Colin, so we know it'll be a thorough job.'

'Although a somewhat depressing one,' muttered Gerry glumly.

Colin Winter had been awarded his nickname of Cold Colin not through his surname, but because he was considered as cold as one of his own cadavers. Still, even though he was not exactly a bundle of laughs, he was very thorough. Apart from the Fenland Constabulary's senior Home Office pathologist, Professor Rory Wilkinson, Cold Colin was undeniably the best forensic pathologist they had in the county.

'The other downside is that he gives nothing away until every test he can think of has been run.' Kate sighed. 'And at times like this, I'd really appreciate a few educated guesses.'

As they watched the scene-of-crime unit offload their equipment, ready to photograph, search, collect and secure any forensic evidence, Kate marvelled at how things had changed over the years. Working the scene, and evidence recovery, had become more like a military exercise. Gone were the days when detectives could get in first and have a good shufty around. Now, they were obliged to don all-in-one protective suits, masks and overshoes. She felt mildly cheated at having to stand back and wait until some masked individual summoned her to her own crime scene.

'I suppose I couldn't leave Cold Colin to you, boss?' asked Gerry hopefully. 'I'd like to grab a few words with Chick, in case he gets called back to the station.'

Kate threw her a knowing look. 'Nice one, kid. But why should we both suffer? I'll fill you in later. Go and talk to Chick, and double-check that neither Chick nor his crewmate recognised either the driver or the licence.'

'Will do, and thanks.'

Gerry was gone in a nanosecond, leaving Kate smiling to herself. She didn't blame her DS, in fact if there had been someone else to offload the job on, she'd have done the same. She took a deep breath and went to greet the stony-faced pathologist.

* * *

Gerry found Chick at the cordon tape. She liked the older man, respected his long years in the force. Experience was something that couldn't be taught. Moreover, in the changing world of policing, he had hung on to the right values. Plus, he reminded her of her favourite uncle, sadly now deceased. That alone made him a good guy in her book.

'Are you and the other officers who took the shout absolutely sure you've never seen the dead guy before, Chick? Or the face on that bogus licence?'

Chick shook his head. 'Complete stranger, DS Wilde. I had a good look, and even though the poor bugger was covered in blood, I could see he wasn't anyone I've ever had any dealings with. We all agreed on that.'

'What about his licence? Anything there strike you?'

Chick wasn't quite so quick with a reply to this one. 'You know what driving licence photos are like; they're grainy, and they all look like mugshots. But the name meant nothing, and from what I could see, the face didn't ring any bells either. It was clearly not our man, unless he'd shed twenty years, and had had a perm and a facelift.'

Gerry smiled. 'And what's your take on the car? You said all the identification marks had been obliterated — do you think that was done by the killers before they topped matey-boy and shoved him in the ditch?'

'No,' said Chick instantly.

Surprised, Gerry asked him why.

'The removal of that engine number. It had been gouged off ages ago, it wasn't recently done. We can't check the chassis number till they get the body out, but I suspect you'll find it's the same. The car is a dog. Frankly, I doubt we'll ever trace the owner.'

Which means no clue to its dead occupant, thought Gerry. Looks like we really do need Cold Colin on this one.

* * *

Kate had tried every trick in the book, including being official, then very nice, to try and extricate a few comments about the deceased man from Cold Colin. All to no avail. All she received was the usual comment: 'It'll take as long as it takes, you can't rush thorough forensic tests. I don't work on assumptions or guesswork, DI Carter, as you well know.'

'And as you well know, I was only hoping for a professional overview of the scenario, Colin, nothing more.'

She knew it was a hopeless task, but Kate wasn't one to give up easily.

'Okay, two small things,' said the pathologist suddenly. 'He wasn't killed very long before he was dumped in the car and ditched. And that neck wound wasn't caused by the windscreen. That's all you're getting.'

Kate had to stop her mouth falling open. Colin *never* told you anything, let alone information like that. For one moment there she could have sworn she had seen the hint of a fleeting smile on his tight lips.

'Uh, well, thank you,' she stuttered. 'I appreciate that. I'll look forward to your preliminary report.' Shaking her head slightly, she left him to do his job undisturbed, and went to find Gerry.

'You okay, boss?' asked Gerry.

'Just suffering from shock. Cold Colin actually told me something, and I'm still trying to get over it.' She smiled. 'He says that head wound didn't come from hitting the windshield, and he reckons he was killed shortly before he was deposited into the ditch. He certainly wasn't murdered hours beforehand.'

'Blimey! That's a first. I see now why you looked so shocked.' She screwed up her face. 'Though it only confirms that he was murdered, and we knew that.'

'And it confirms it's one for the Serious Crimes Unit,' Kate added. 'Right, well, let's hope Colin can clean him up well enough to get some good post-mortem images, then we'll run them through facial recognition. You never know, he might have had his collar felt for something in the past.'

'He's not known to Chick, so he may not be local. Still, the PNC would pick him up, no matter where he came from,' said Gerry.

'So, it's back to base and we'll get the ball rolling,' said Kate, wondering where this case was going to take them. Like Gerry, she had an uneasy feeling that there was more to this than met the eye.

CHAPTER TWO

Barney Capstick considered his landlady, Miss Enid Houghton, to be a thoroughly unpleasant woman. She was stick thin and had the tightest lips he'd ever seen, along with piercing eyes that bored clear into you. Her permanent expression was one of suspicion. He saw her once a week, to pay his rent, as did everyone else living there. He hated those trips up to the top floor, and escaped as soon as he possibly could. If he'd been able to find somewhere else to live that both suited him, and that he could afford, he'd have buggered off months ago. Nevertheless, beggars couldn't be choosers. At least he had a roof over his head. He was forced to smile. And what a roof it was. Standing in acres of grounds, Knighton House was a rambling old property that had once been a grand family residence owned by landed gentry, possibly even nobility. Somehow the family had diminished over the years, finally coming down to the only surviving member, Enid Houghton. It seemed that the money had diminished too, as the old lady had been forced to bastardise the elegant old house, and had split it into flats, apartments, bedsits and anything else she could think of to claw back enough money to keep it going. Even the stable block, barns and outbuildings had been turned over to small businesses, repair shops and one-man bands who were prepared to rough it in order to earn a crust from their labours.

Barney wasn't a particularly fussy man, but his little flat was about as basic as it was possible to be. And it was damp. The heating system was antiquated, and he couldn't afford to use plug-in heaters. The one real advantage to living here was the fact that Miss Houghton had allowed him, for an extra few pounds a week, the use of a small area in the stable block to store his equipment. Barney was a gardener, and needed somewhere for his mower and various other pieces of gardening paraphernalia. He could also park his old van right outside his store, which helped a lot when he was loading up ready for work.

Barney sighed. Sadly, work was out for the next week. He'd strained his back helping a friend out with a bit of hard landscaping. Now he was supposed to be resting, so as to avoid any ongoing problems. This was bad news; he needed the regular money. However, he also saw the sense in backing off temporarily and taking care of himself. The doc had advised painkillers, gentle exercise and short walks, but absolutely no lifting. Well, at least he had the grounds to walk in. Oddly, old lady Houghton allowed all her "paying guests", as she liked to call them, access to the entire six acres of garden. He was surprised she didn't charge them for the privilege, she was that mercenary, but for some reason it didn't seem to worry her to see them walking the overgrown paths and even sitting on folding chairs on the unkempt lawns.

Barney liked the grounds, but it pained him to see the state they were in. There were days when he was tempted to get out the mower, the strimmer and hedge cutter, so as to make at least one area look good again. He could see from the planting, the old trees and the general layout that back in its heyday, the gardens at Knighton House would have been superb.

Barney made himself a hot drink and wondered how he was going to pass a whole week in this place. He loved his work and was good enough at it to have built up a small group of regulars, some of whom had become friends. Being stuck here would be hell. He sipped his tea and decided that he needed something to occupy his mind, a project of some sort. Nothing too energetic, nothing that would injure his back further, just something to prevent him climbing the walls.

Barney stared at his laptop, frowning. He wasn't into computer games. He wanted something to engage his brain, not atrophy it.

He sat for a while, mulling over possibilities. Family history? That could be interesting. His flat had remarkably good Wi-Fi, which always surprised him, considering that the area was notorious for its weak signal. Maybe he could start a family tree.

Barney stared out of the window, eventually focussing on a weathered, overgrown stone lion that had once sat proudly on a plinth, standing guard over the wide steps that led up to the main front doors. For a moment, he saw it as it had been, and knew exactly what he would do with the next week. This place, for all its pitfalls, fascinated him. He would trace the history of Knighton House and its once beautiful gardens. He would walk the grounds and look with fresh eyes at the architecture, and mainly at the garden design. He might even try to map the complete estate, visualise it as it was. He could search out some archive pictures. Maybe he could steel himself to speak to the old dragon herself, and ask her about the history of her home.

Barney smiled to himself. Suddenly the thought of a week off didn't seem that bad at all.

* * *

Colin Winter stared at the selection of items retrieved from the car in the ditch. It certainly was a mix. Some of the objects were mundane and to be expected, like windscreen scrapers and a tyre pressure gauge. He also saw shopping bags, and assorted cloths, tissues, a notebook and pens. Others were more unusual, like a small hand saw, and an old shoebox filled with small plastic bags. One thing that stood out from the rest was an old forty-five rpm record that he'd found in the glove box.

Colin peered at it through the plastic evidence bag. 'Parlophone,' he whispered to himself. 'That's a record from the sixties.' He recalled his father's huge collection of LPs, EPs and singles. He recognised the group. Retro pop music? It certainly didn't accord with the cocaine residue they'd found in that odd Continental tyre. This was a bit of an enigma. And something he would take great delight in imparting to DI Carter. This little puzzle would really pique her interest. He gave a rare smile. Despite himself, he liked DI Kate Carter. She had a brain that ran along the same lines as his own. She was shrewd, and very observant — he got the impression that very little escaped her. Colin was glad that she was handling this one, and for her, he'd make an effort to wring every possible bit of evidence he could from both car and body. He had enjoyed her look of total amazement when he'd surprised her with a few snippets of unexpected information at the site.

He left the collection of artefacts and returned to the body.

'Are we ready to begin?' he asked.

'Everything is prepared, sir,' said Jimmy Flynn, his senior technician. 'Ready when you are.'

Colin now had his work face back in place, the one that had earned him the nickname of Cold Colin. He knew what they all called him, but then they knew nothing of his history, and why he lived only for his work. Without that, he would probably disintegrate. He made no friends — he didn't dare — and he dreaded the day that someone would be kind to him, ask him how he was, how he *really* was. He might then, in a moment of weakness, consider answering them. If that were to happen, he would never stop crying. The fact was that in the entire division, the only person he felt the slightest bond with was DI Carter. It was irrational, he knew that. They barely spoke, other than about official business, but he still felt a connection with her.

'Sir? Can I make the initial incision?' Flynn was looking at him curiously.

'Get on with it, man,' he snapped. 'We have a Serious Crime Unit waiting on our report.'

***

Kate stared at the old whiteboard in the main investigation room, and wondered how long it would be before it was replaced with a new, all-singing, all-dancing interactive version. Technology was taking over, and although she certainly was no Luddite, she aimed to hold onto her good old-fashioned whiteboard for as long as she could.

Old or new, the whiteboard held precious little information. To the location of the car, and photographs of it and its occupant in situ, she had added a few observations, including the fact that the dead man was a murder victim. Now she had to wait for Cold Colin to give her his report.

Gerry came and stood beside her. 'Hell, I hate this bit. Waiting never was my forte.'

'Use the time to consider what we do have,' said Kate. 'Then, when the forensic tidal wave hits us, we won't be swamped by the details. Now, have we had anything in from uniform yet? Anyone seen in that area prior to the finding of the car?'

'Chick said there was only one report of a dark-coloured four-by-four, seen by a woman whose son works a night shift at a food processing factory. She thought she heard an engine, and assumed that he had come home early. When she looked out, she saw a vehicle she didn't recognise, driving very slowly towards the spot where the car was found.' Gerry shrugged. 'Not much, is it?'

'I'm thinking it could have been a pick-up vehicle, gone to collect whoever drove our dead guy out onto the fen. Once he'd gone into the ditch, the killer — or killers — would have needed wheels to get away. Did the woman give Chick a time?' she asked.

'Just before five in the morning,' said Gerry.

Kate nodded. 'Mmm, kind of ties in, doesn't it? Considering when the car was spotted. We'll see what time of death Colin gives us and try to link this vehicle to the crime. I suggest we get someone to check the cameras for a dark four-by-four on the main road around that time. An Automatic Number Plate Recognition camera might just give us a few hits to check out.'

Gerry went off to organise that, and Kate was left staring at the wreck of a car, the dead man behind the wheel. 'Who are you?' she whispered softly. 'And what did you do to get yourself killed so brutally?' But no answer came.

She heard her office phone ringing. 'DI Carter, you will find post-mortem photographs dropping into your inbox any moment now. We've done our best with him, and hopefully it's enough for you to use with the facial recognition programme.'

'Thank you, Colin, and I appreciate how speedily you've got these to me.'

'The preliminary report will be with you by close of play, but tox reports can't be hurried, as you know. Oh, and we are already running his DNA through the database; hopefully that will be of some benefit.'

Kate thought he sounded less officious than usual, and after he'd so uncharacteristically given her some information on site, she began to wonder about Cold Colin. 'That's good news indeed. He might well have fallen foul of the law at some point.'

There was a short pause, and then, instead of his usual curt goodbye, Colin said, 'If you have a few moments, I suppose you couldn't drive over here? We've removed everything from the crashed vehicle, and there's something that doesn't make sense to me. I thought you might want to take a look at it.'

Unlike the Fenland Constabulary's main forensic science laboratory and mortuary facility that was based in Greenborough Hospital, Colin Winter worked from a small but highly specialised mortuary unit in the grounds of what had been the local cottage hospital. It was only a couple of miles from the station. Deciding not to ask for details of whatever had puzzled the pathologist, Kate said, 'I'll head over now.'

She pulled on her jacket and called from her office door to Gerry, who was walking towards her. 'I'm off to the mortuary. Colin is puzzled about something found in the car.'

Gerry raised her eyebrows. 'From that odd tyre?'

'I've no idea, but I will soon see. I'll be back within the hour.'

'Want me to come?' asked Gerry.

'No, I'm fine, this won't take long. Oh, and are the cameras being checked for that four-by-four?'

'They're working on it now, boss. Chick says he's spoken to the owner of the driving licence that was found on our dead man. He says it was in a wallet that was stolen from him two weeks ago in one of the local pubs.' Gerry shrugged. 'Our man could be a tea leaf, in which case, he should be in the police files. Or do we think we're that lucky?'

'Probably not, we can but hope.' Kate grinned. 'Hold the fort, Gerry, I won't be long.'

Fifteen minutes later, Kate found herself staring at an old forty-five record.

'Of course you may think you've had a wasted journey,' said Colin flatly, 'but I suspected you might have the same feeling I did when I set eyes on that old disc.'

'Yes . . .' murmured Kate. 'I have no idea of its significance, but it's certainly set those warning bells ringing.'

'I know that feeling well. I get it during post-mortems sometimes; a strange nagging in my brain telling me to look further into what could be a perfectly harmless little growth or abnormality. It's never wrong.'

Kate was not used to this Colin. He was speaking with her like a human being, and she was afraid of saying something to upset this new understanding. She decided to act as she would with anyone. 'They call it "copper's nose", but I believe it's just years of experience. When we're doing a job we love, we develop an awareness of when something isn't as it should be.'

'I'm sure you're right,' replied Colin. 'And, please, when you solve this crime, do let me know the significance of that.' He pointed to the record.

She looked closer at the Parlophone label, and immediately recognised the 1960s pop group. 'The centre of the record is missing,' she mused. She heard a soft chuckle.

'That's because it's from a juke box — you know, the kind they had in cafés back then. You could pick up cheap records, because when they updated their selection, the old ones were sold for peanuts. You bought little plastic centres that clipped in, and they'd play a treat on your record player.'

Kate looked at him incredulously. 'How on earth do you know that?'

'I grew up with a record collector for a father. He had hundreds of forty-fives, and a lot of the rare ones he picked up were without centres.' He pointed to the black disc in the evidence bag. 'I could sing every word of hundreds of sixties and seventies songs by the time I was eight. But don't worry, I won't burst into song right now.'

Kate marvelled at how he said all that but managed to keep a poker face. 'Then I certainly will keep you informed about the meaning of our little artefact from the past. And thank you, Colin. I'm very glad you showed me this.'

He nodded curtly. 'All the other data will be in my report. I've fast-tracked it, so I won't keep you waiting too long. Now, I have other work to attend to.'

Kate thanked him again and returned to her car, her head spinning. Never, in years of working on cases that Colin had handled, had she heard him offer anything other than forensic facts. And he'd certainly never laughed.

Scratching her head, she drove back to the station, wondering why on earth an old retro pop record would cause two professional people to have their intuition jump to high alert.

CHAPTER THREE

That night, after the children had gone to bed, Kate, still mulling over both the record and the apparent defrosting of Cold Colin's attitude towards her, was cuddled up with Tom on the sofa watching an old black-and-white film. However hammy the film might be, it was a means of unwinding and enjoying some closeness without the kids.

When the phone rang, they both groaned.

'Oh no, please, not work again.' She sighed.

'I'll go and make tea,' said Tom, jumping up. 'Then if you have to dash, at least you'll have had one decent cuppa.'

Kate picked up the phone, but for a moment there was silence. 'Hello?' she asked impatiently. 'Who is it?'

'Kaa-tie. Kaa-tie.'

The sing-song voice had an eerie, sibilant quality that made her freeze.

'Who is that?' she demanded.

'Kaa-tie. Kaa-tie,' the creepy voice sang again. Then the line went dead.

Tom stuck his head around the kitchen door. 'Not work then? Wrong number?'

For a moment she couldn't answer; she was still hearing that insidious voice repeating her name. Then she stammered out, 'Uh, n-no, not work.' She grabbed the receiver and dialled 1471. As she expected, the caller had withheld their number.

Now Tom was by her side. 'Talk to me, angel. Who was that?'

'I don't know, but he freaked me out. He, well, he was *singing* my name, over and over.' She tried to copy him, but it didn't sound nearly as threatening as it had.

'What a bastard!' exploded Tom. Then he calmed instantly and hugged her. 'Come on, babe, this isn't like you. You look really upset. Normally you'd be swearing your head off and consigning him to the hottest part of hell.'

'I guess I was expecting it to be work, not some nutter. But he has our home number, Tom, I don't hand that out to all and sundry. Neither do you. And he called me by my name.'

'Babe, you of all people know how easy it is to get information these days,' reasoned Tom. 'A few taps on a keyboard, and if you know what you are doing, you can access practically anything.'

She knew he was right, but she felt totally spooked. Then she remembered the note under her windscreen wiper that morning. She told Tom.

'Oh shit! You've got a stalker.' He looked aghast. 'What did you do with the note?'

'Screwed it up and tossed it on the drive. It's probably still there.'

In an instant, Tom had switched on the outside lights, grabbed a torch, and was hunting up and down the drive. 'It's not here,' he called to her. Then hurried back inside, and locked the door. 'And this morning's note was the first? You've never had anything like that before?'

'No, nothing. I'd have told you. And I didn't give it a second thought. Hell, we have a murder case running, I honestly thought no more of it.' Now she was getting angry, a good sign. 'It's probably some arsehole I banged up years ago, who has just got out and is after a bit of payback. Goodness knows I've upset enough villains in my time, I really shouldn't be surprised.' She said all that, but in her heart, she knew this was different.

'Okay, babe. I'll finish making that tea, and we are going to sit and talk,' said Tom firmly. 'At some point, some man must have shown interest in you, even if it didn't register too much. We'll see if we can weed him out.'

Kate nodded, although she had a suspicion that this kind of man stayed in the shadows and never made contact. Even so, she was grateful for Tom's positivity. She told herself for the millionth time how lucky she was to have such a wonderful, caring husband. From their first day together, Tom had been a rock, in so many ways. He respected her work, and he adored his family — enough to leave a well-paid job in Peterborough and become an outworker, working from home. Overnight, it seemed, he had assumed the roles of house-husband, child-minder and chef, while still turning over an impressive salary as a creative graphic designer. Kate had always marvelled at his ability to simply accept things and make them work.

For the next hour they talked, Tom asking sensible questions to which she could find few answers. The fact was, no one had flagged up warning bells, or shown an unhealthy interest in her.

'No one's attitude to you has changed recently?' asked Tom, stifling a yawn.

'Unless you class my pathologist actually being helpful for the first time in his life, no,' she said. She saw the suspicious crease in her husband's brow, and laughed. 'No, darling, it's not Cold Colin. He simply found an anomaly in this murder case and considered it worth sharing. The opinion of another professional was all he wanted, since it bothered him. I honestly think poor Colin is incapable of getting close to anyone. He's a workaholic, lives for his career, and I swear he's no stalker.'

'Then I think we've exhausted all the possibilities, babe. Sorry it wasn't much use.' Tom stood up. 'Let's turn in, shall we? It's late.'

Kate agreed. She felt mentally drained, having run the gamut of emotions. Shock, fear and boiling anger had hit her, one reaction after the other.

As they settled down to sleep, with Tom's arms protectively around her, she said, 'This is so unlike me, darling. He freaked me out, damn it, he actually scared me. I've been threatened with knives, and even a shotgun. I've faced up to druggies off their heads on crack cocaine and walked into more dangerous situations than most people have had hot dinners, but this guy . . .' Words failed her.

'Try to sleep, babe. I'm sure that tomorrow, in the cold light of day, you'll feel very different.'

She hoped he was right, but as she finally drifted off into an uneasy slumber, she kept hearing, 'Kaa-tie. Kaa-tie.'

* * *

Some miles away from Kate's village, a man lay fully clothed on his bed. He had not undressed as he had a job to do in just over an hour's time. He checked his phone and decided he could afford a short nap.

The main light was off, the curtains tightly closed. The only light came from a single bulb in an anglepoise lamp. It stood on a chest of drawers at the foot of the man's bed and shone up onto the far wall, where it lit up a framed photograph. It was poster-sized, and glowed, alive with colour in the lamp's beam. It was the head-and-shoulders image of the most beautiful woman in this man's world. Without taking his eyes from the picture, he drifted into a light sleep, singing softly to himself, 'Kaa-tie. Kaa-tie.'

CHAPTER FOUR

The following morning saw the usual bedlam of getting the animals and the kids fed, and the latter organised for school. Eddie wanted to be in early to meet a new pupil and introduce him to the breakfast club. From what Eddie had told them, this boy never had a proper breakfast at home like they did, and he felt sorry for him. Tom and Kate were hardly going to complain about their son helping a disadvantaged child, so Tom needed to be on the road an hour earlier than usual. He was now heading off with a vehicle full of children, a good fifteen minutes before she was due to leave.

Left alone, Kate's thoughts returned to her stalker, if that's what he was, and she felt a tiny pang of uneasiness. For the first time, she had an inkling of what being a victim felt like. She had talked to so many women, and occasionally men, who had been terrified by the attention of such a predator. Now she started to appreciate their fear for herself.

With an angry shake of her head, she gathered herself together. She must not let this arsehole get between her and her investigation.

Ten minutes later, after double-checking that the house was locked up, Kate went out to her car.

She was a few yards away from it when she noticed something, and her eyes narrowed. Balanced on top of the front wheel on the driver's side, just under the wheel arch, was a package.

She approached it with caution, and with mounting irritation. What the hell was it this time? Close inspection showed it to be a small box of handcrafted Belgian chocolates, wrapped with a ribbon and a gift card.

Kate grabbed it. The card simply said: *Kate. Your favourites.*

And they were too; the ones that Tom gave her on birthdays and anniversaries.

At that point, anger took over from common sense, and the red mist descended. She marched back to the side of the house, opened the refuse bin and hurled the package in, taking great delight as it landed with a squish amid the leftovers of last night's pasta and meatballs.

All the way to the station she silently fumed and cursed this unwelcome intrusion into her life, but Tom had been right — well, partially. The Kate who arrived at work, immaculate as ever, and completely in command now that she was in her own working environment, was not the shrinking violet of the night before, or the angry harridan of earlier. Even so, that simple singing of her name, over and over, kept haunting her. Then the foolhardy act of binning those chocolates, when she should have brought them in and had them checked for fingerprints, dawned on her. With a curse, she texted Tom and asked him to fish them out of the rubbish and place the box in a clean plastic bag. She vaguely hoped that the spaghetti sauce had not done too much damage.

After her first coffee of the day, and a careful appraisal of the overnight reports, she prepared for a morning update with her team. After that, she decided, she was going to talk to Arun about her stalker. Superintendent Arun Desai was not only her boss, but her friend. They had gone through basic training together, and she had always admired his work ethic, and his compassion for victims of any kind. Apart from being a sympathetic ear, he needed to know if one of his officers was under any kind of threat.

'Boss!' Gerry hurried in through the door without stopping to knock. 'We've got a name for our John Doe!'

Kate looked up in surprise. 'Tell me!'

'He is Stephen James Clarke, and he's from a village just outside Holbeach, so not from our patch. The DNA database came up with a match.'

'So, is he known to us?' asked Kate.

'Used to be a bit of a bad boy. Nothing too serious, mainly petty crimes, but then he seems to have decided that crime doesn't pay — he's been clean for over three years.' Gerry placed a report in front of her. 'He found a regular job with a local company, and that was definitely not his car. He has — sorry, *had* — a Citroen C3.'

'So, what did he do to get himself murdered? And who did that wreck of a car belong to?' Kate frowned. 'Colin found a residue of drugs in that odd tyre. I've got his prelim report.' She looked at Gerry. 'Give me a few moments to look through this, then go and get Tony and Luke, and tell them to grab us all a coffee, then I'll fill you all in on the forensic findings so far.'

Ten minutes later, the four detectives were gathered around the whiteboard. Kate was happy to see considerably more information on it now, especially a name for their dead man. She hated the expression John or Jane Doe; it seemed somehow disrespectful. The dead should always have their proper name.

DCs Tony Sharpe and Luke Harcourt had been with Kate for almost five years, and along with Gerry, they made about as close a team as it was possible to get. She knew it couldn't last; both men could sail through a sergeant's exam if they wanted, but right now, Kate simply appreciated the team that she had.

She read them the contents of the file about Stephen Clarke, noting that he was twenty-seven years old and lived alone in a small cottage, two doors away from his parents' house, in Fleet St Michael, about two miles from Holbeach. 'Gerry and Luke, I'm giving you the unenviable task of notifying the parents, and when you think it's appropriate, you need to ask them if they knew of anything he was involved in that could have led to his death.'

The two colleagues glanced at each other, grimaced, and then nodded. It was all part of the job. Not a nice part, but a necessary one, and Kate knew it was something they could handle very well. Both officers were diplomatic and compassionate, but equally competent at gleaning important information from bereaved families.

'I'd have gone myself, guys, but I need to see the super as soon as possible.' She halted, undecided as to whether to mention the stalker to her team. Maybe she should. They would be best able to watch her back if need be.

She told them, expecting a few jokey comments, but none came. They all looked deadly serious.

Gerry Wilde was the first to speak. 'That is one crap thing to happen, boss. Have you any idea who it could be?'

Kate sighed. 'None whatsoever. But it's the reason I've bailed out of going to see the Clarke family; I need to make the super aware I'm under some kind of threat.'

'Absolutely,' agreed Luke. 'And don't worry about the Clarkes, we can handle that.'

She knew they could. Luke was in his late twenties, and had a boyish, likeable face, topped with a mop of dark-brown hair, full on top and cut short at the sides and back. In his dealings with the public he came across as trustworthy and honest, and he always got the best from witnesses and victims.

Tony — mid-thirties, stocky, with very short, prematurely greying hair — was Luke's polar opposite. He was quiet and his expression never gave anything away. Extremely perceptive, Tony had the ability to spot a liar at fifty paces. Something the criminals never got to see was his wicked sense of humour. Kate could only imagine what Tony must have been like as a schoolboy.

'Has Tom fished that chocolate box out of the bin yet?' Gerry asked her. 'We might be able to trace where they were bought, or even lift a dab, unless the meatballs have really done a number on it.'

Kate took out her phone, but there was no message from him. 'He's probably not back yet, he was supposed to be popping into the supermarket on the way home. I can't believe what a prat I was to chuck it away. It was just the thought of that creep hanging around our home, it made me furious.'

'Understandable,' said Tony.

'But not very professional,' she said. 'I don't usually get riled up like that.'

'It's an invasion of your personal space, apart from the weirdo side of it,' said Luke. 'I know what I'd like to do to the slimeball.'

'After I've got to him first,' said Tony darkly.

Kate felt a rush of affection for her team; suddenly she didn't feel so vulnerable. Vulnerability wasn't a feeling she normally associated with herself, but somehow that horrible sing-song voice, repeating her name, had got to her, and she couldn't shake it off.

'If there's anything we can do,' said Gerry, 'just say, and we'll be there.'

Tony and Luke both murmured in agreement, and Kate felt a lump forming in her throat. 'I really appreciate that, guys. But right now, I need to update Arun, and you'd better go and see the dead lad's parents. We'll meet up again when you're back.'

* * *

Barney had risen early and was out walking the grounds of Knighton House. He guessed there were parts of the garden that he had never even seen before. So often he worked late, when there weren't many daylight hours left for exploring. The trouble with gardening was that you were governed by the weather. He had suffered through days on end when constant rain had made it impossible to cut grass, or even weed. Typically, now he was unable to work, the weather was fine.

Barney followed the doctor's instructions to the letter, in order to get back to work as soon as possible. He had a bit put by; he wouldn't starve. Trying not to think too much about the lack of income, he concentrated instead on his new project. Today, he was walking the boundary, so as to gauge the size and shape of the rambling grounds. He'd done some background research on Google, but the place was so overgrown that it was very hard to work out where it began and ended. He'd already discovered a tiny folly, so well-hidden that he'd never come across it before. Somewhat resembling a chapel, the little hexagonal structure seemed to be without purpose, until you went inside and saw a glassless picture window that would have provided a view of the lawns and flowerbeds. Today, the lawns were unkempt and the flowerbeds had almost disappeared beneath a covering of weeds and rampant shrubs. Looking through the window, Barney pictured it as it had been, and made a few notes and pencil drawings in his sketchbook.

'It must have been splendid in its day, mustn't it?'

Barney jumped. He had believed himself to be alone out here. He turned to see another tenant, a man who inhabited one of the ground-floor flats.

The man laughed. 'Beg pardon, young man, didn't mean to startle you.'

Barney smiled a little sheepishly. 'I was miles away. It would really have been something, wouldn't it?'

'Well, you should know. You're that gardening chappie from the second floor, aren't you?' The man held out his hand. 'Arthur Montgomery, or if you want to be formal, *Major* Arthur Montgomery, retired. Pleased to meet you.'

'I'm Barney,' he said, taking the hand. 'Barney Capstick.'

'Ah, Capstick. Splendid name. Hails from Lancashire or Yorkshire, I believe. Means a woodcutter. But I expect you knew that.'

'No, I didn't. And my family originally came from the North Yorkshire Moors. How did you know that, Major Montgomery?'

'For heaven's sake, do call me Arthur. English surnames have fascinated me since I was a boy. Bit of a passion, really. Hear a name I'm not familiar with and I have to check it out.' He chuckled. 'Nice to have a passion, isn't it, even at my age.'

Barney agreed, and they stood in silence, gazing at the expanse of tangled greenery.

'You have an interest in this old place then?' asked Arthur.

'Kind of. I hurt my back laying paving slabs, and I've been told to rest for a week. I can't just do nothing, so I thought I'd try to do a bit of research on the house — well, the grounds mainly — and try to fathom out what they would have been like back in its heyday.'

As he spoke, it dawned on him that he'd never spoken at length with any of his neighbours. They were a far from sociable bunch!

'Perhaps I can help you?' offered Arthur. 'I started doing the same thing not long after the wife and I moved here. Mind you, my interest was the house, rather than the garden. I felt almost duty-bound to know something about the place we were living in.'

'You said "started". Did you give up on it?' queried Barney.

'Wife got ill, lad, found myself in the role of chief cook and bottle-washer. The old duck pulled through all right, but my research remains where I left it, stuck in a box file in the bottom of my wardrobe.' Arthur shrugged. 'I can dig it out if you like.'

Barney smiled at him. 'If it's not too much trouble, that would be great, thank you.'

'My pleasure, young man. Tell you what, come and have a sherry with us before lunch. Twelve o'clock. Apartment Two. I'll retrieve my findings from their hiding place and hand them over then.'

Arthur left him to continue his walk, wondering as he went if any of the other tenants of Knighton House were as amicable. Maybe he should actually speak to them and find out. Meeting Arthur had made a big difference to how he thought about the place. If the damp could be sorted, it really wasn't that bad.

Fifteen minutes later, all thoughts of making his flat more homely flew from his mind. He opened a rusty wrought-iron gate and entered a wooded glade. He initially assumed it to be a pet cemetery, until he realised that some of the markers were old and ornate. Further in, he came across full-size headstones, most bearing the name Houghton. He had found the family burial ground.

'Well, who'd have thought it?' he whispered to himself. He pulled his phone from his pocket and took several photographs. The folly had been quite a find, but this was even better. Looking around, he suddenly realised that this was the only place in the garden where the grass had been mown; a neat path led off between the gravestones, its edges clipped and tidy. Barney frowned. Someone still came here then, to look after the graves. The only person he could think of was Enid Houghton. Maybe her parents were buried here. Or maybe she considered it her duty to keep her ancestors' final resting place in some sort of order.

If that was the case, she wasn't doing a very good job of it, because most of the stones were covered in moss and overgrown. He stared at the path, then began to follow it. It didn't take him long to discover its purpose.

A little way from the other memorials stood a white marble headstone. In a stone vase in front of it, fresh white roses had been placed.

When Barney drew nearer, he was surprised to see that, although it wasn't a recent addition, it was spotlessly clean, and instead of the usual inscriptions, it bore a single name, Amelia, with a delicately carved rose beneath it.

He shivered. He was trespassing, and had no right to be here. With one more glance at the grave, he turned tail and hurried out of the cemetery. A glass of the Montgomerys' sherry suddenly seemed like a really good idea.

* * *

Before Kate went upstairs to the super's office, she checked her phone for messages and saw one from Tom. When she opened it, it read simply, *Call me when you can.*

She rang him immediately. 'Sorry, sweetheart,' he said. 'I got your message but I think I might have misunderstood.'

She frowned. 'I only wanted you to get that chocolate box from the outside bin and bag it for me. What's the problem?'

'Then I didn't get it wrong. Sorry to tell you this, Kate, but it's not there. There's no box of chocolates in our dustbin.'

CHAPTER FIVE

Superintendent Arun Desai listened without interrupting. Then he stood up, telling her to wait for a moment, and went out of the office. Kate heard him just outside, talking to his secretary.

A few moments later he was back. 'Before you arrived, I'd been talking to the force psychologist, Professor Julia Tennant. I've asked Helen to stop her before she leaves. I think we could do with an informed opinion on this stalker of yours.'

Kate was considerably relieved, both by the fact that Arun had taken it seriously, and that there was a professional on hand who might give her some clue as to what this man was all about, and what she could expect next. At this thought, various nasty scenarios began to play out in her head.

They were lucky to have Julia Tennant as force psychologist. Kate knew something of her background; formerly a highly respected university lecturer, she had a worldwide reputation in her field. Why she had chosen to work with them was an enigma, to Kate at least, but no one was complaining. For her part, Kate was always slightly in awe of her.

She walked in, a tall, elegant woman, almost stately, with short, silver-grey hair and a sharp, intelligent gaze.

She smiled at Arun. 'You can't get enough of me, can you?'

'Sorry,' he said, 'but something's come up that needs your expertise. DI Carter here has attracted a stalker.' He turned to Kate. 'Maybe you can explain what has been occurring.'

She related the events of the past couple of days, along with her thoughtless act of discarding the chocolates.

'I very much doubt that they would have helped,' said Julia. 'He would most likely have worn gloves when handling them, but it is disturbing that he saw fit to remove them from your bin. Clearly he was watching you from somewhere, and that definitely needs investigating. How do you get on with your neighbours?'

Kate considered this for a moment. 'Our immediate neighbours are great, we are all good friends. The others — well, we only talk in passing, but they seem okay. It's a decent neighbourhood, and people generally look out for one another.'

'Then pick the ones you really trust, tell them about your problem, and get them on board.' She smiled. 'A good curtain twitcher can be invaluable, as you probably know.'

'Having heard what Kate has told you,' said Arun, 'is this man following a pattern? And if so, where is it likely to go? Should we be considering taking action — officially, I mean? And what can you tell us about stalkers and their mindset? We usually just get to clear up the aftermath.'

'Oh my! So many questions.' She turned to Kate. 'First, I have to say how sorry I am, my dear. In my opinion, drawing the attention of a stalker is one of the most upsetting things that can happen to a woman — or a man for that matter. Even if it doesn't pose a serious threat — and they don't usually cause actual physical harm — it has a profound effect on the person being stalked.'

'You can say that again,' said Kate. 'I'm generally tough as nails, but hearing that weird sing-song voice, just, well . . .'

'I can imagine. It's a horrible thing to happen. Anyway, you must be totally focussed from now on. You need to record every single thing he does — times, dates, and a description of his actions. And keep everything. Throw nothing away.' Julia looked to Arun. 'I think you should take this very seriously. Mainly because Kate is a detective inspector and will have made a lot of enemies during her career, and one of the things that can drive a stalker is revenge.' She shrugged. 'Not that I'm totally convinced that's the case with this man, but we cannot take any chances.'

'So, what do you believe is the case, if it's not revenge?' asked Arun.

'Stalking is all about a desire to exert control over a victim. From what Kate has said, because of the wording on the first note, and the gift of chocolates, I'm beginning to suspect that this man has a fantasy that he has a relationship with our Kate. It's entirely in his mind, and it's a little like celebrity stalking. After all, Kate is a powerful woman, with a high-profile job.' She turned back to Kate. 'And as you can think of no former lover whom you spurned, or someone whose advances you might have turned down at some point, this man has a fantasy about you, and wants to bring that fantasy to life.'

There was one question that Kate dreaded the answer to. 'Is there any likelihood that he could pose a threat to my family?'

'Let's not get ahead of ourselves, Kate, it's early days yet. He might even move onto someone new, especially if he realises that things are becoming too hot for him. It could also be an infatuation, and he'll give up when he realises it's fruitless. Let's take it a step at a time, shall we? Up security and get the neighbours on board. Do you have any security cameras?'

'No, we've talked about it, but as I said, it's a nice road with friendly people, so we never really saw the need. Besides, I see so many security cameras in my job, I didn't want to go home to one, and we wanted our children to feel safe without having to stare at a screen in case there's a bogeyman in the garden.' Now, of course, she was regretting that decision.

'I can put a car outside to warn him off,' suggested Arun. 'Then if he was just testing the waters, he might well back off.'

Kate suddenly felt a rush of anger at this man who was intruding on her precious home life. She was about to object, but thought of Tom and the children. She had a duty to do everything possible to deter this creep, and if it meant having a police car parked outside for a while, then so be it. 'Okay, Arun. If you could organise that, I'd appreciate it.'

Eddie, at least, would enjoy having it there.

***

The man stared at the box of chocolates. It sat on a wad of kitchen paper in the middle of his table. He had carefully wiped away the tomato sauce and straightened the ribbon.

It was a shame that she had acted that way but he had expected as much. She would soon start to understand that he was not just some lovesick lonely heart, but a man who was deadly serious about her. Deadly serious.

***

By a quarter past twelve, Barney was on his second sherry and revelling in the good company. In fact, he had rarely felt so welcome anywhere. Furthermore, their lovely apartment bore no trace of damp.

Arthur had presented him with a battered old box file brimming with documents, pictures and computer printouts, all relating to Knighton House.

'Of course, we've known Enid for donkey's years,' said Arthur's wife, Lottie, offering Barney a piece of homemade butter shortbread. 'I expect you think she's a bit of an old battleaxe, but underneath that hard exterior, she's a very kind person.'

Moderating the reply that nearly rose to his lips, Barney admitted that she did seem rather unfriendly.

'All a front, old boy,' said Arthur. 'Woman had a tough life, you know, and this old pile — well, I have no idea how she manages to keep it going. Place is a veritable money pit.'

'We were her first PGs — paying guests — you know.' Lottie smiled at him. 'Originally, our apartment was the library and reception room. After we moved in, Enid spent quite a bit on refurbishing the ground-floor rooms so as to make two apartments and three smaller flats, so we were lucky. As time went on, she realised that she needed a lot more money coming in, but the funds for major work were just not available, so she had to resort to minimal expenditure.'

Barney looked around at the elegant room, at the ornate ceiling and big open fire, and grimaced. He himself, he said, was living in one of the "minimal expenditure" flats with a shared bathroom, and he was battling the damp and poor heating.

The Montgomerys regarded each other in dismay.

'Oh, dear me,' said Lottie. 'That's not good for you at all. I had no idea they were damp, did you, Arthur?'

Arthur shook his head. 'I knew they were pretty modest, but I didn't realise they were that bad. Perhaps I could pop in and take a look? I'm happy to have a word with Enid for you if you think it might help.'

Barney shook his head. 'You are welcome to come and look anytime, Arthur, but please don't say anything. If she were to put my rent up to cover the cost of any work done, I just couldn't afford it. It's my fault for not buying adequate heaters.'

After a moment or two's silence, Arthur suddenly sat upright. 'Well, if that's the case, there might be another solution. There's a small flat down here on the ground floor. It's clean and warm, and has its own bathroom. I happen to know that the man who lives there is planning to move out shortly as the company he works for is relocating. It would be more expensive, but I've got an idea to solve that.' Arthur's expression was that of a game show contestant who knew he had the right answer to the million-pound question. 'What say you give old Enid a few hours a week in the garden free of charge? That would cover the extra rent. And I know we could swing that one for you.'

'Oh yes,' said Lottie excitedly. 'You may not think it, but Enid is heartbroken about the grounds being so overgrown. She used to have a gardener, just for the lawns and the beds nearest the house, but the money ran out.' She looked quite cross for a moment. 'And I don't like that man in Flat One, I'll be very glad when he's gone.'

'Oh, he's all right, my dear. Eric's just a bit antisocial, that's all,' said Arthur. 'His only friend here is an odd cove who lives on your floor, Barney. He has one of the flatlets on the side of the house. I think his name is Paul, but don't hold me to that.'

'I think I know who you mean,' said Barney, picturing the big, burly man with cropped hair and the nose of a retired boxer. 'I've passed him on the stairs a few times but he never speaks, even if you say good morning to him.'

'That's the one,' said Arthur. 'Rude as they come. Not like our neighbour. Eric's not exactly chatty, but he does acknowledge a greeting.'

'I still don't like him,' Lottie said firmly. 'It would be so much nicer to have Barney as a neighbour.'

'Do you think Miss Houghton would agree?' asked Barney. This could be the answer to everything. Better living conditions, and he'd still have somewhere for his van and gardening equipment. Oh, and a bathroom of his own. Bliss! How many times had he got home from work, desperately needing a shower, only to find someone camped out in the bathroom.

'We'll lobby her in a two-pronged attack, won't we, old girl?' said Arthur.

'We will. And she'll say yes, I'm certain of it.' Lottie beamed happily.

'Well, I'd be really grateful for that, and I could certainly put aside some hours to tidy up the garden. In fact, it would be a pleasure to get it looking good again.' He looked at Arthur. 'You know this place much better than me, did you know there were family graves in a copse at the far end of the grounds?'

'Oh yes,' said Arthur. 'Like a lot of these old country families, the Houghtons of Knighton House always buried their dead on their estate.' He sat back. 'There's a good deal of interesting history about burials on private land, you know. In some places, the ground needed to be consecrated, and in others it didn't. Planning permission was often required too, but not in grounds like this, since it's not close to other people's property. There would have been no restrictions where this place is concerned.'

'I found it this morning.' Barney hesitated. 'It seemed so private that I didn't feel I should linger, but there was one grave that stood out; it had the name *Amelia* on it, and there were fresh flowers.'

Arthur and Lottie glanced at each other, and then Lottie sighed. 'Amelia was her granddaughter, Barney. And before you tell me that Enid isn't married, that's true, but she did have a child, and Amelia was her only grandchild.'

'How sad. Did she die young?'

'Nineteen years old,' said Arthur, 'and we don't know the details, because Enid has never been able to talk about it. It was a tragic accident of some kind, and we've never had the heart to pry.'

'Her grave is well cared for,' added Barney. 'Is that Miss Houghton?'

'Oh yes,' said Lottie. 'She goes there twice a week and cuts that grass with an old hand mower, and trims the edges with shears, all by herself, despite her arthritis. Won't let anyone help her.' She sighed. 'That girl dying almost finished her off. She aged ten years overnight.'

'So please don't mention it when you speak to her, Barney,' said Arthur emphatically. 'As you will, if we negotiate this move down here.'

'I wouldn't dream of it,' he replied swiftly, and meant it. He had known the moment he had walked down that neatly cut path that he was in an intensely private place, and that he had no right to be there. Unless invited, he would never set foot in that burial ground again.

CHAPTER SIX

Just as Kate was starting to think about lunch, Superintendent Arun Desai came into her office, looking rather anxious.

'I have a favour to ask, Kate.'

'Fire away, Super.'

'There's another body been found on the fen.' He held up his hand. 'It's okay, I'm not throwing a second case at you, it's just that DCI Smithson is up at HQ today. It's going to be his baby, but I wondered if you'd take one of his team and do an initial appraisal and liaise with forensics. Cold Colin is already there, so I'm told.'

'Of course, I'll go immediately.' She had decided that the best way to keep her mind off her stalker was to keep working. 'Location?'

'Ancombe Farm, Back Lane, Ancombe Fen. It's about four miles out of town on the Greenborough Road.'

'I know it,' she said, whisking her jacket off the back of her chair and checking the pockets for her car keys. 'We did a witness statement in Ancombe last month. I've got this, don't worry. What do we know so far?'

'A farmer by the name of Barclay was overseeing the demolition of an old barn, and he found more than mouldering hay bales and rotting potato sacks. A youngish, female victim, not a recent death by the sound of it, but that's all we have.' Arun patted her shoulder. 'Thanks, Kate. I owe you one.'

'A proper coffee and a Belgian bun would do me fine.'

'I got off lightly then. I'll have it for you on your return.'

As Kate drove, she wondered what sort of mood their pathologist would be in this time. She didn't hold out much hope for further juicy bits of information, just that he wouldn't be as chilly as he could be sometimes.

Her travelling companion was a detective constable called Trevor Lennox, who was known to be taciturn. Today, however, he seemed positively chatty.

'I've had a quick check through a list of local missing persons — young females reported missing in the area during the past few years, but it's impossible. There are so many of them. I need something more specific, or I'll be wasting my time.'

Kate agreed. The misper list was terrifying. Thousands of people went missing every year; around 170,000 of them in the UK alone. 'Let's cross our fingers that she has either some identification on her, or a distinguishing feature.' Kate was thinking particularly of the tattoos that were so popular these days. 'It would be nice to give your boss a name when he gets back from HQ.'

'Huh,' Trevor said. 'Knowing him, he'll expect us to have not just a name but a complete history, a rundown on how she died, *and* who did it!'

Kate merely smiled. DCI Ian Smithson was an impatient man who did a great deal of shouting. In her opinion, yelling at them was not the way to get the best out of your officers.

Ancombe Farm was clearly undergoing a lot of major work. Several large outbuildings were being demolished and had been cordoned off behind security fencing. Kate noted the tractors with backhoe loaders, an excavator, along with various other pieces of equipment scattered around. One of these sites was also surrounded by police and CSI vehicles.

She parked a little way from the confusion and, noticing all the mud, looked down at the sergeant's feet. 'I don't give your trainers much of a chance of surviving that lot, Trevor.'

'Nor your smart black shoes, DI Carter,' he said.

'Ah, but I have wellies in the back of my car,' she said smugly. 'And luckily for you, a pair of my husband's left from the last dog walk.'

They didn't fit too well, but Trevor was grateful. Boots on, they trudged across to where the landowner and a uniformed officer were waiting for them.

'We've been planning this for years,' said Patrick Barclay. 'We used to have livestock on the farm, but the year before last we went over to just crops, and we needed better storage for the heavy equipment. We were just about to get rid of those old barns when this happened.' He sighed, pointing to where the SOCOs were moving in and out of one of the partially demolished buildings. 'My son found her. He was clearing out all the old hay and the like, ready for the 'dozer. To think that poor kid has been lying there unnoticed for so long, it's just horrible. My wife is in bits over it, and I've never seen my son so upset.'

Kate assured the farmer that they would move her out as quickly as possible, but unfortunately all work would have to cease for the time being, as it was now a crime scene. She was sure from his shocked expression that he had nothing to do with it, but even so, she'd met some very accomplished liars in her time. Everyone working on that farm at the time of the girl's death would have to be investigated thoroughly.

'Well, I'd better go and take a look for myself, sir,' she said. 'We'll keep you updated.'

She and Trevor made their way over to the cordon, signed the log and ducked underneath. There they pulled on the obligatory coveralls and masks.

Colin Winter looked up as they approached and raised an eyebrow. 'We meet again, DI Carter.'

So he was still in a good mood. 'We have very little detail so far, Colin. Just that it's a female and she's been dead a while.'

'More than a while, I'm afraid. More like two years; the body is partially mummified.'

More information. Kate was liking this new Colin, not wintry but tepid.

'She's been wrapped in a thick layer of sacking, and hay was heaped up around her, hence the mummification. Even so, it's not pretty.'

Beside her, Trevor, who had obviously never heard Colin utter more than a few terse words, was staring at the man, open-mouthed. Stifling a giggle, Kate beckoned to him and they followed Colin to where she lay.

The pathologist had already removed the sacking, exposing the body, which was part skeleton and part brown leathery skin, although a few blonde curls still clung to the skull.

'Oh my. I see her clothes are still more or less intact,' Kate whispered. 'The colours have faded and some of the material is threadbare, but they are quite distinguishable.'

'Different materials decompose at different rates,' Colin said. 'Man-made fibres take longer. Pure linen can biodegrade in as little as two weeks, but polyester can take anything from twenty to two hundred years.'

'I never knew that,' said Kate, having never really thought about it before. 'That's a suede jacket, isn't it? And a very distinctive shirt. That could certainly help in identifying her.'

'She has a ring too,' said Trevor, indicating a bony finger. 'And I think I can see a necklace. That's quite a bit to go on.'

'She's not a youngster, is she, Colin? Maybe not even a teenager?'

'No, not a girl,' he said, 'more like a young woman. Mid-twenties maybe? Now, if you've seen all you need, I must get on.'

Kate thanked him and they retreated into the fresh air.

'Bloody hell, DI Carter. Respect. You get along a whole lot better with Cold Colin than my boss. He's dead rude to Smithson.' Trevor was amazed.

Kate laughed. 'He's usually dead rude to everyone. He seems to have had some kind of epiphany. He's been almost friendly for two days now. I'm as surprised as you, believe me. Long may it last.'

'Can't see it extending to the DCI; I reckon you're just lucky. It makes life a whole lot easier, and—'

Before Trevor could finish, a SOCO came running out of the barn behind them. 'DI Carter! Can you come back please? The pathologist wants to see you. Alone, if you don't mind.'

Kate frowned. 'Hang on here, Trevor. I've no idea what this is about, but I'll fill you in, don't worry.' She hurried after the SOCO.

'Colin? Is there a prob—?'

She stopped and stared. In Colin's gloved hand was an old forty-five record.

'It was under her jacket,' said Colin after a while. 'The label has all but disintegrated, but you can just see it's a Pye — I can tell by the pink colour, and there's a tiny bit of text left. It's another well-known group from the sixties, but the name of the song has gone completely—'

'And the centre is missing,' concluded Kate. 'What the dickens connects a fresh, possibly gang-related murder to one committed a couple of years ago? This is madness.'

She wondered what Arun would say when she told him that, contrary to his assumption, the two cases were very much connected.

She eyed Colin hopefully. 'I shouldn't ask this, but can you speed this through? This was supposed to be DCI Smithson's case, but it now seems to be mine. We have a definite link between the death of Stephen Clarke and this young woman, and it'll be down to me to find out what the hell these records mean.'

'I was about to say I'd prioritise this. *You* need to handle this, DI Carter, not that great ape Smithson.'

Ignoring that last comment, she said, 'Thank you, I appreciate that. And one more thing. That record, and the other one, are obviously at the root of these crimes, and since you know more about them than I do, will you help me to try and discover every possible thing about them?'

'Of course. And once again, I was just about to offer.' The corners of his mouth twitched — almost a smile. 'I still have an old record player at home, and some plastic centres. I'll bring it in to the lab and we can play them. Sometimes the clue is in the lyrics. Music, often those special tunes, can be very emotive.'

He was right. Kate thought of the countless couples who had a special song. She and Tom had one; they had played it at their wedding. She still went all soppy when she heard it. Yes, Colin was right. Music was a powerful thing. They needed to hear those lyrics. She could find the Parlophone song online, as they had the title, but this one needed to be played to identify it.

'Call by the mortuary tomorrow, and I'll have the record player set up,' said Colin. 'And I'll be able to give you a rough report of my findings. Make it the afternoon though, as it will take time. Given the state of the corpse, it'll be a few hours before I can get it back to the lab.'

'I'm sure it will,' Kate said. 'I'll let you get on, and thank you for your help.'

Back with Trevor, she told him of Colin's strange find, and the connection to her current case. With every word, the amazement on his face increased.

'That is so weird! I can't make head nor tail of that.' He bit his lip. 'Er, DI Carter, do you think I could get seconded to your team to help on this one? You see, the thing is, I'm thinking of putting in a request for a transfer. I love my career, and I love the Fens, but I'm struggling with DCI Smithson. I've been with him two years now, and, well, I've had enough.'

Kate understood perfectly. She herself wouldn't have lasted two days with that rude man. She now saw why Trevor Lennox was often uncommunicative and sullen. The Trevor who had accompanied her to Ancombe Farm was another person entirely. 'I can't promise, Trevor, but seeing as how our workload just doubled, and that you've seen the crime scene with me, I'll speak to the super and see what I can do. We can certainly use you, but as you know, the decision will be down to politics.'

'I can't ask for more than that. Thank you, DI Carter.'

Driving back to base, Kate realised that for a whole two hours she hadn't even thought about her stalker. Nevertheless, she was still terrified of what might lie in store for her at home.

CHAPTER SEVEN

The working day was ending when Superintendent Arun Desai heard a soft tap on his door.

'Julia! I thought you'd have been long gone by now.'

The psychologist gave him a weary smile. 'No peace for the wicked. I was just about to leave when I had a call from your custody suite. They had a distraught man in the cells who was demanding a crisis team, and of course no one was available except me.'

'Poor you. Have a seat. Can I get you a restorative coffee? Tea?'

'I suppose your machine doesn't dispense Scotch, does it?' She smiled. 'A coffee would be good, thank you. White, two sugars.'

Arun arranged for two coffees to be brought, and resumed his seat. 'So, why the return visit? As if I didn't know — Kate Carter?'

'Yes, the lovely Kate. I'm troubled by what she told us, Arun. The thing is, she is a very attractive woman, and in the eyes of many people, a powerful one. She is a prime target for an obsessive, fantasist stalker. What worries me the most is that call to her home, and that he sang her name in that terrifying way.'

'That really gave me the creeps when she described it,' Arun said.

'You do have a car outside her house now, don't you?'

'Yes, it'll be there twenty-four seven until I pull them out. Apart from the fact that DI Carter is my best officer, she is also a friend. And on a professional level, the Serious Crime Unit deals with a number of complex cases. If she were to become inattentive or too distressed, mistakes could be made.' He frowned. 'That sounds a bit harsh, but in my position, I am forced to see the bigger picture.'

'You are just being practical, Arun, which is perfectly understandable,' said Julia. 'And talking of mistakes, have you considered the motive for this sudden interest in her? It may seem a bit devious, but maybe someone wants to remove her from an investigation she's working on.'

They waited as their drinks were brought in, then Julia continued. 'I assume that if the situation got worse, you would insist she leaves whatever she's working on and passes it to another team?'

'I would have to if her work was suffering. Besides, she would probably insist on it herself. She's a perfectionist, and a bloody good detective. If she thought she wasn't giving a hundred percent to her work, she'd ask for leave until it was cleared up.' He sipped his coffee. 'Do you really think that's what is behind this?'

'It would be a very effective way of messing with her mind, that's for sure,' said Julia grimly. 'In my professional life I've come across any number of sick and damaged people, but stalkers are among the most concerning. It's the insidious way they insert themselves into a person's life. The stalker is not out there on the street randomly waving a gun. He is after *you*. No one else. And he is always there, following, watching. It is terrifying. The victim becomes phobic. I'm telling you, Arun, the attentions of a serious stalker can crack the toughest nut. Some end up unable to sleep, some have nightmares, and others succumb to depression or post-traumatic stress.'

'You believe that Kate's man is serious then,' Arun said quietly.

'I'm afraid so. I didn't want to scare her in case I'm jumping the gun, but I have a very bad feeling about this. That's why I came back. She may need help, mainly from you. However, as it happens, I'm staying with a dear friend in Saltern-le-Fen this week, so if I'm needed, I will make it my business to be on hand.'

'That's good to know,' said Arun. 'And if we do bring any suspects in, I'll make sure you get to see them first.'

After Julia had gone, Arun sat in the quiet of his office, ruminating. He too felt uneasy about Kate being the focus of unwanted attention, and at a time when she had a double murder investigation running. His mind wandered to what she had told him earlier about the cases being connected. It seemed inconceivable, but it couldn't be dismissed. A man is brutally murdered, placed in an old car and driven into a ditch, and a pop record is found in the car's glove compartment. Then, the day after he is killed, a woman is found. Having been murdered, she lies in sacking and under hay, in the back of a disused barn, for two years. Beneath her jacket is an old pop record. Arun shook his head. Coincidence? No way! So, what the hell was going on?

* * *

It had been a relief to get home and see two uniformed officers that Kate recognised in a marked car outside her house. They acknowledged her as she parked her Sportage, and she had promised to make sure they were well supplied with tea.

Inside, Tom was looking harassed, while doing his best to keep the children occupied and trying to prevent Eddie from staring out of the front window, waving to the police officers and making a noise like a police siren.

'We need to talk, babe,' he said, as she hung up her coat. 'I've told the kids that as soon as they've eaten, they can watch a movie. Then you and I can talk without little ears picking up anything we say.'

She agreed immediately. The children, and what to say to them, was her main priority.

'I hope you don't mind but I've cheated on dinner tonight — not that the kids are objecting,' Tom said. 'No home-cooked meal this evening, I'm afraid, it's coming courtesy of Deliveroo.'

'Family feast?' she asked hopefully, thinking of one of the local restaurants which was particularly good.

'It certainly is, plus burgers and chips for the guys outside.'

'Oh lord, we'll never get rid of them now,' she said with a smile that soon faded. 'I just wish they didn't have to be here at all. What have I done to deserve this?'

'Nothing, babe. Absolutely nothing.' Tom hugged her. 'Other than captivate some bloke with your dazzling good looks, and since that's exactly what you did to me . . .' He kissed her forehead. 'Let's hope he takes one look at that car outside and decides to bugger off.'

He was trying to keep it light, but Kate knew that deep down he was as worried as her, maybe more. She believed they had one of the most successful "police" marriages ever, but then there weren't many husbands like Tom.

Before they tied the knot, they had discussed the problems that might arise from her career. There were risks; you didn't do a job like she did and return home every evening, smiling and happy, unscathed by what the day had thrown at you. There would be sacrifices, she warned, and compromises, mostly on Tom's part, but he had accepted them all, saying merely that life would be boring without a few challenges, and that anything would be better than life without her.

On her part, she never burdened Tom with the darker side of her work. She would discuss things that puzzled her, ask his opinion, and tell him the funny stories, because there were many. People, especially petty criminals, some coppers too, did very silly things sometimes. As the years passed and the children had come along, she had got separating work and home down to a fine art. It was as if there were two different Kates, and she left the one that dealt with evil, damage and death in her office at the station. Now this pervert had come along and blurred the lines she had drawn, and she hated him for it.

After the meal, and with the kids settled down to watch *Paw Patrol: The Mighty Movie* for the umpteenth time, Tom and Kate went into the kitchen, where Tom poured her a glass of wine and took a beer from the fridge.

'Okay, where do we stand with this creep?' Tom asked.

She wished she knew. She wished she could tell him something positive, but there weren't any positives. Instead, she told him what Julia Tennant had said, along with Arun's reaction.

'I'm glad he's taking it seriously,' said Tom. 'Unlike some of your high-ranking officers who are only concerned with the costs.'

'He has to be careful, because of the job we do. We upset a lot of people during an investigation, and not just the one we bang up at the end of it. He's very aware that this could be more than just a lonely bloke with a misplaced crush on a policewoman.'

'And what do you think?' Tom asked.

'I think I've never been so rattled, or so goddamned angry at someone,' she said. 'We've worked so hard to find a balance between my job and keeping a happy and safe home for our children, and now this bastard has waded in and muddied the waters.' Tears sprung into her eyes, but they were tears of frustration and anger. 'As far as I'm concerned, he's trespassed on sacred ground, and he's going to pay for it.'

Tom looked taken aback. She rarely spoke like this at home.

'There's still a chance that he's just that lovesick bloke you spoke of earlier. He hasn't actually threatened anyone, just left a note and a gift — oh, and made that phone call. Now that was creepy, I admit.'

'Yeah, and to make it he needed our private number, didn't he? And he retrieved his unwanted gift from the bin,' said Kate. 'And I don't think he wanted it back as a present for his mummy, do you?' She took a long swallow of wine. 'I have bad vibes, darling. Sorry, but there it is.'

'I know, and sadly, so do I,' said Tom. 'So, how do we play this? What do we tell the children? They're bright enough to pick up on how stressed we are.'

'At present, they think the police car is there because I said they could use our house for a training exercise, right?'

Tom nodded. 'Yep. I told them exactly what you said, that those men are being trained in observational skills, and they mustn't worry if they see police officers checking the garden, even if it is late. It's all part of their training.'

'Then we'll keep to that. Meanwhile, all we can do is wait, and be prepared for what comes next. This guy will either back off, because we have taken measures to get rid of him, or I'll get another gift. Or something.' Kate didn't like to think what that "something" might be. 'Oh, and the home phone is going to be bugged as soon as Arun can arrange it. Calls in will be recorded, and hopefully traced back to the caller.' She drank more wine, and then leaned across to take Tom's hand. 'I know you won't let the children out of your sight, but can you extend that caution to the animals as well? I've seen some pretty gruesome things happen to pets when someone is out for revenge. Our pets are our family, we can't have him getting anywhere near them. I swear to God, if he hurt Rodders, or Del Boy, or Trigger, not to mention the moggies, the duck and the tortoise, I will personally tear him limb from limb!'

'Only if there's anything left after I'd finished with him,' said Tom darkly. 'I've been thinking about this all day. If we have one more thing happen, and there is any indication of a threat to anyone or anything, the children go to my mum and dad, and I'm sure your brother will have the dogs, as he loves them to bits. As for the cats, I guess it's the cat hotel for them. Brian has his winter pen in the conservatory, so I can get that sorted in no time, but Matilda is a problem.' He frowned. 'I don't know anywhere that boards ducks.'

'Tony Sharpe's wife would take her. She has rescue chickens, and several ducks of her own. She knows more about ducks than I do, and I know she'd help out if we needed her to,' said Kate, picturing the pens, ponds and little houses scattered around Tony and Julie's garden. 'I don't want to think like this, but we have to make provision for the worst-case scenario. I just pray it never comes down to that.'

'Expect the worst and hope for the best, isn't that what your mum always says?' Tom said.

'It's all we can do. But one thing, babe. Promise me, no heroics. We have no idea what we're up against, and if he is out for revenge, he won't be someone you can reason with. In that case, he will probably be a hardened criminal, and you are too precious to get hurt. And if it's someone mentally unstable, well, who knows what they'd do?'

'And that goes for you,' he said. 'You have no idea how scared I am that my beloved wife is being targeted by some nutter. What's more, you're out of my sight all day. If it goes on much longer I swear I'll be a head case.'

'If we didn't have this bizarre murder case running, I'd take leave immediately. Though thinking about it, it's me he's after, so the further away from you and the children I am, the safer you'll be. And I'm surrounded by coppers all day. He's hardly likely to wander into the police station to offer me a bunch of flowers.'

Looking at his glum face, she said, 'And if it does get serious, I will take leave. We'll do as you suggest with the kids and the animals, and we'll weather it together. Deal?'

Tom nodded. 'Deal. But I can't promise not to knock seven bells out of him if I ever see him!'

* * *

As the church clock struck eleven and somewhere an owl screeched to its mate, the man lay in bed, his eyes wide open. He pondered the way apparently random events seemed to come together to form a pattern. Who would have thought that a difficult job — one that he'd almost turned down — would have brought him to her door. Thank goodness he had taken it on. Obviously, it was meant to be. What was more, after a few more visits to her home, she would work it out. He wouldn't even have to pursue her, smart detective that she was. She would come to him.

Given that she was acting exactly as he had expected her to, he decided to reward himself. He'd take tonight off, maybe tomorrow too. He could do with the rest, as his day job was pretty exacting. He would be sorry not to see her, but needs must.

He gazed at the picture on his wall. Needs must.

CHAPTER EIGHT

At eight thirty, Kate was sitting in Arun Desai's office nursing her second cup of coffee of the morning. 'All was quiet last night; he didn't show at all.'

'I'm not surprised,' said Arun. 'He'll either be regrouping and deciding where to go from here, or he'll have given up.'

'Or maybe he was expecting this reaction,' said Kate. 'He will know I'm a detective, so it was a predictable next move to have officers on obbo outside my house.' She gave Arun an anxious look. 'And he'll also know that our budget won't permit us to keep that situation going for much longer. Everything hangs on whether he's a serious stalker, or a chancer.'

'Well, for now, they stay, so don't worry about that.' He smiled at her. 'You are a highly precious commodity in this unit, and an old friend, so I shall ensure that my budget accommodates you as long as I dare.'

Arun told her that Julia Tennant was going to be staying in the area for a while, and would be available should she be needed. Kate liked Julia, and respected her work, so that was very good to know.

'I've got another favour to ask, Arun, if you can pull it off for me. Any chance of me borrowing DC Trevor Lennox for the two murder investigations we are running? I could certainly do with the extra manpower, as we have double the work to do now. Plus, he seems very interested in the cases; he was well up to scratch at the crime scene yesterday.'

'You forgot to mention that DCI Smithson is not exactly getting the best out of him at present,' Arun added dryly.

'Er, yes, that is another issue, I admit, but not really mine to pursue. I was thinking of the smooth running of this operation. I need extra help, and as Trevor was present at the first examination of the body, I thought . . .'

Arun held up his hand. 'Enough said. I'll square it with Smithson. I'm fully aware that Lennox has the wrong temperament to work with the DCI — or should that be the other way around? I get the feeling Lennox will be asking for a transfer in the not too distant future. He does have the makings of a very good detective, so we'll throw him a line for the duration of this case, and then see how things pan out.'

'Great! He'll be over the moon. Thanks, Arun. It looks like I owe you another one. The way we're going, I'm going to be permanently in debt to you.'

As she stood up to leave, Arun said, 'Just don't let your guard down, Kate, not for one minute. I know you're going to be up to your neck in these cases, but spare a minute or two to think about any old threats, or villains that might have long memories.'

'So, you reckon this is down to revenge, not some guy with an out-of-control crush on me?' she asked.

'I'm covering all bases,' he said. 'Just stay alert and make sure you report every single event.'

'Oh, I will,' she said. 'Believe me.'

***

Having presented in great detail to Enid the advantages of allowing Barney Capstick to have the room on their floor when it became free, Arthur and Lottie Montgomery waited expectantly for her response.

'He would love to help bring some life back to this garden, Enid,' said Lottie enthusiastically. 'And I have no doubt that he will do even more hours in a week than would cover the extra payment. He's desperate for a little more comfort — and no damp.'

Enid frowned. 'Oh dear, I really do need that extra cash for Mr Payne's flat when he leaves. This place is draining me. I'm sorry that young man's room is a little damp, but that part of the house has always needed more heat. We thought it was a leaky gutter, but it's something to do with the roof, and costly roof work is simply beyond me. But it would be so nice to see the garden looking cared for again. It was really beautiful once. Oh dear, oh dear.'

'Come on, old girl!' said Arthur cheerily. 'Give the lad a break. Just think how good it will feel to look out and see a freshly cut lawn and neat flower beds again. It'll be worth it. He loves this garden. And that means he'll do a good job. What do you say?'

'I can't deny it would lift my spirits. Seeing it the way it is just breaks my heart,' Enid murmured. 'All right. I'll give him three months' trial from when Eric Payne moves out. Let's see if it works for both of us, and in the winter months, perhaps he can do a few odd jobs to cover the extra rent.'

'There are always things to do in a garden, even in winter,' said Lottie. 'Our old gardener worked all year round when we had our house. But I'm certain Barney'll be happy to do any odd jobs that he's capable of.'

'I'll speak to him when he brings his rent,' said Enid. 'And if I feel I can trust him to not cheat me, the flat will be his when Mr Payne leaves.'

'Do we know when that will be?' asked Arthur.

'Less than two weeks,' Enid said. 'He gave me official notice yesterday. Apparently, his company has already relocated to Kettering, but he is tying up loose ends on an unfinished job. I understand he already has new accommodation in place.' She sighed. 'I'm losing two of my paying guests at the same time, I'm afraid. Another gentleman is going on the same day. He works at the same company as Mr Payne, but he isn't going with them. He's going to work with his brother down in the West Country.'

'Would it be that rude cove on the first floor?' asked Arthur hopefully.

'Ah, Mr Paul Ricketts. He isn't exactly friendly, is he?' admitted Enid. 'Still, we never know what goes on in other people's lives, do we?'

In Arthur's opinion he was just pig-ignorant, but he kept that to himself. Now he knew why they were seen together a lot.

'Well, my dear, I'm sure you'll soon get new tenants — I mean paying guests,' said Lottie. 'There are so many people looking for affordable places to live these days.' She smiled at Enid and raised an eyebrow. 'And to be honest, Mr Payne and Mr Ricketts aren't exactly a bundle of fun, either of them, are they?'

Enid pursed her lips. 'We shouldn't judge people when we don't know their circumstances, Lottie. I try to distance myself from the private lives of my guests as much as possible, with the exception of you two, of course.'

And how well she does it, thought Arthur. He'd often had occasion to overhear the "guests'" acid comments about their landlady. New blood in the old house would be welcome, and it looked like young Barney would get a warmer home too. Well, win-win, as the youngsters said.

* * *

The sound of pop music coming from a mortuary was somewhat incongruous, especially when it was Cold Colin acting as DJ. Kate giggled. Maybe she'd stepped into a parallel universe.

'Ah, DI Carter. As you may have heard, your record has suffered no ill effects from its two years in the clutch of a dead woman.' Colin lifted the arm of the old Dansette record player and placed it back at the start of the song. 'It was released in the same year as the first one: 1964. Both records were in the Top Ten, though they featured different artists singing in different styles, and were produced by two different labels.'

She listened to a group hammer out a fast dance number. It had to do with drowning the sorrow of a lost love in the beat of rock and roll. She determined to print out the lyrics as soon as she returned to her office. There could be a connection somewhere, although the first record had been a love song, much gentler, though quite catchy.

'Thanks for that, Colin,' she said, as the record came to an end.

'I'm afraid the date is the only connection that I can see, but you might pick up on something I missed.' He handed her a sheet of A4 printer paper. 'The lyrics to both records.'

She thanked him again. It seemed they were thinking along the same lines. 'You managed to get the woman out of that barn and back to the lab all right?'

'It wasn't an easy task, but yes, she's in one piece, and we've had a preliminary look at her. She was stabbed, once, in the back. We are about to start the post-mortem, but already I can see from the location of the wound that the blade penetrated between the ribs, punctured the lung and pierced the heart. If that is so, it wasn't merely luck on the part of the killer. They knew exactly what they were doing.' He gave her a long look. 'That killing was carried out with military precision.'

Kate stole a glance at Colin's assistant, Jimmy Flynn, who had been regarding his boss with mounting bewilderment. Seemingly, this Colin was new to him too.

'I'll leave you to carry out your autopsy then, Colin, and I look forward to reading your report.' She indicated the record player. 'And thank you for bringing in that little piece of history.' Again, she caught that slight upward curve of the lips.

As she closed the door behind her, she heard him bark at Jimmy. It seemed the thaw extended only as far as herself. Better make the most of it then, thought Kate.

* * *

'Can we help you, Super?' asked DS Gerry Wilde, catching sight of their superintendent at Kate's office door. 'The DI is still at the mortuary, sir.'

'Good,' he said. 'It was you I wanted to talk to, actually, and Sharpe and Harcourt, if they're around.'

Luke was at his desk, Gerry saw, but Tony was missing. 'Where's Tony?' she called.

'He's in the throne room, Sarge,' said Luke.

Just then Tony reappeared, and Gerry beckoned to them both. 'Super wants a word, fellas, grab a couple of chairs.'

'Now,' Arun began, 'DI Carter. I expect she has told you about her stalker.'

They nodded.

'Good, I thought she'd have mentioned it. I wanted to let you know that I'm taking it very seriously. Between us, I'm certain it's related to her work. Someone is out for revenge. I'd like to ask you to cast your minds back and see if you can come up with anyone who might wish to threaten DI Carter.'

'We've been together as a team for years now, sir, so we're the right people to ask,' Gerry said. 'We'll put our heads together and see if we can come up with any likely candidates.'

'I was banking on that,' said Arun. 'It's a lot to ask, I know. You are run off your feet with the current cases, but maybe you can do some ferreting into the old ones. I think it goes much deeper than some random guy with the hots for DI Carter.'

'We discussed keeping an unofficial watch on her home, sir, but then you sanctioned a car, so we backed off. I think I can speak for all of us when I say we'll do our best, even outside working hours.' Tony and Luke nodded.

'The boss has been good to us, and she's also a damn good detective,' said Tony, 'and we can't wait to get our hands on this guy.'

'That's what I was hoping to hear,' said Arun. He got to his feet. 'And keep this to yourselves for a bit, would you? The last thing I want is to cause her more worry, especially if I'm being over-cautious. I'm sure you know what I mean; we see so much bad stuff in this job that it's hard not to assume the worst.'

Gerry turned to the others. 'Okay, lads. Suppose we meet up in the Old Oak after we've finished for the day, and then we can work out a plan. What d'you think?'

'Good idea, Sarge,' said Luke, 'especially if the first round is on you.'

CHAPTER NINE

At six thirty that same evening, the three detectives were nursing pints at a secluded table in the main bar of the Old Oak.

'Our main problem is how far back do we go,' Gerry began. 'Some villains have long memories, and old grievances can fester if you're stuck in a prison cell.'

'It doesn't even have to be the criminal themselves,' added Luke. 'It could easily be someone on the outside who resents the DI for banging up a loved one. Remember that woman whose husband died in prison? She went after DCI Smithson in a big way; she even sprayed his home in graffiti. Blamed him for everything.'

'Oh yeah,' chuckled Tony. 'She conveniently forgot that her beloved husband had killed a man, and that he got topped in prison for double dealing a drug dealer.'

'This is different, I reckon,' said Gerry.

'How come?' asked Luke.

'I don't know.' She sighed. 'To me this feels more like the work of a psycho. Most of the people we put away are rough types, usually not very bright. Take your angry wife. She acted just as I'd expect — out there in the open, waving her spray can and yelling obscenities. I can't imagine her singing down a phone like DI Carter said her stalker did. Oh, and he managed to trace her private number.'

'So, if it's not some hard man, who is it?' asked Tony. 'What kind of person should we be looking for?'

'"Think outside the box", as the saying goes,' Gerry said. 'Disregard the thugs with the big mouths and look for someone who really disturbed us. Maybe the boss has mentioned someone she found especially unnerving, as in creepy rather than thuggish.'

'More Hannibal Lecter than Rambo,' said Luke.

'Norman Bates, more like,' added Tony grimly.

Luke laughed. 'What? You mean this guy wants the DI sat in a rocking chair for decades, so he can talk to her dead body?'

Gerry took a gulp of her beer. 'You may laugh, but that could be exactly the kind of thing he wants. You know, get her tied up somewhere, totally incapacitated, and keep her there, all to himself.'

'Shit, Sarge,' said Tony. 'And the super was afraid that *he* was overreacting.'

'Okay,' she said, 'maybe that's stretching it a bit, but look at what he's done. That first note, saying how beautiful a woman she is, had been carefully written, not scribbled. What's more, when her husband went out to retrieve it, it had gone, and she said there was no wind that day. Then there was that creepy sing-song voice on the phone, repeating her name. The third thing was the chocolates — and they weren't just any old ones, they were her favourites. What's more, the bastard said he *knew* they were her favourites. Finally, he gets them out of the bin. So he had to've been watching her when she winged them.' She looked at her companions. 'This man is clever; he's no common criminal. He is targeting her where she's most vulnerable — her home.'

'Yeah, that's a point,' said Tony. 'He hasn't gone near her when she's been out and about, like in the supermarket car park or somewhere. And he's really pushed the right buttons, hasn't he? I've never seen the boss so rattled.'

'I think he's barely started,' added Luke gravely.

A glum silence fell, broken by Tony. 'Yeah, but that's only one angle. He could still be a perverted creep, a stalker with sex on his mind. That's scary enough.'

'So where do we start, Sarge?' asked Luke.

She drained her glass. 'We'd better do as the super asked, and see if we can identify anyone who's threatened her in the past, or that we think might bear a grudge. Though for my part, I'll be concentrating on the sinister creeps.'

* * *

That day, Tom Carter had barely stopped to draw breath. There had been no sign of the stalker, which the officers keeping watch confirmed when he went to ask them.

He had started his day by driving the children to their respective schools — Eddie went to a different one to Chloe and Timmy. He had spoken to their head teachers about the situation, and had been assured that the staff would be informed, and would keep a close eye on his kids. On returning home, Tom went to speak to their nearest neighbours, asking them to please check on the house and garden, especially when he and Kate were out. Bill and Steph Betts, a retired couple who lived in the large four-bedroomed house next door, were flabbergasted to hear the news and promised to be especially vigilant.

Dan Attwood was at work when Tom called round, but his wife, Sheila, promised to tell him as soon as he got home. She too was shocked, and also angry; apparently she herself had fallen victim to a stalker when she was younger. In her case, it had been a boy she had been at school with, who had been obsessed with her ever since. 'It was horrible, Tom. Everywhere I went, he was there. He kept sending me cards and flowers and begging me to go out with him. When he wouldn't take no for an answer, my eldest brother had what he said was "a word with him", although I never asked what that involved. But I spent months looking over my shoulder and imagining all manner of things. Poor Kate! I do feel for her.'

The neighbours alerted, Tom rang an old mate of his who worked in home security and arranged for an outdoor camera system to be installed as soon as possible. His friend said he could install it the following morning. It seemed a bit like shutting the stable door after the horse had bolted, but it was worth the expense. It might at least give them a glimpse of the stalker.

His next job required all the tact he possessed. He had promised Kate that he'd contact their relatives without worrying them. They needed a contingency plan for the children and the pets, even if they never had to put it into action.

After that, he prepared dinner, and then it was time to collect the kids from school. He was relieved to find that both schools had kept the children inside until he turned up. Fortunately, he and Kate always insisted that they must never talk to strangers. Of the three of them, despite being the youngest, Timmy was the smartest at sussing out which people he could trust.

Now Kate was hurrying in through the door. Tom hugged her, wondering where the day had gone. 'Before you ask, all is quiet on the Western Front.'

'I talked to the crew outside before I came in,' she said, casting about for her slippers. 'They've been to all the houses that have a view of our front garden, but the occupants hadn't noticed anything untoward.' She found her slippers in one of the dog beds. 'Ah, good. Cuddled but not chewed. How was your day, sweetheart?'

'Manic, but I did manage to make dinner. Sadly, we can't eat fast food every night. It just needs warming up, so when you're ready . . .'

She hurried off. Soon after, the sound of laughter and barking reached him from above. Tom smiled.

There were times when he wondered how he ever got any work done amid the chaos that was their home, but he did. Did it well, too. He had never missed a deadline yet, and was determined to keep it that way. Now, if he put in two hours tonight, after dinner, while Kate spent time with the kids, he'd have his present project completed and delivered a week ahead of schedule. Not bad for a house-husband currently steering his ship through stormy waters.

Tom heated the food and set the table, something the children normally did. Tonight, he left them with Kate, giving her a little more time with them and a chance to unwind. Humming contentedly, he took knives and forks from the drawer. His own childhood had been a far cry from the happy one his children enjoyed. Abandoned as a baby, he had been passed from hand to hand, finishing up with abusive foster parents. Not the best start in life, but subsequently he'd been adopted, saved by the couple he soon came to call Mum and Dad. Tough as it was, his background had made him the man he was today; a man who would die for his wife and children, who never resented a minute of the time he spent caring for them.

He called out that dinner was ready, and stood aside for the ensuing stampede. Halfway through the meal, he observed that Chloe was being unusually quiet. Amid the stream of chatter, she sat in virtual silence, toying with her food.

'I thought this was one of your favourite dinners. All right, are you?'

The little girl shrugged. 'I s'pose so.'

'What's the matter, little 'un?'

'Mummy doesn't like my picture.'

Frowning, Tom looked across at Kate. 'Picture?'

She shrugged. Clearly, she didn't understand either. 'I love your pictures, darling. What makes you think I don't?'

'Because you took it off the playroom wall.'

'But I never—' Kate pushed back her chair and stood up. 'Carry on with your dinner, I'll be back in a mo.'

'Won't be a sec.' Tom got to his feet and ran after her up the stairs.

In the playroom, they had put up a big magnetic conference board on one wall, so the children could display their artwork from school. Chloe's latest effort, which she had entitled *My Mummy*, was a typical child's depiction of a woman with a round face, a too-large smiling mouth full of teeth, and startling bright yellow hair.

Tom looked at the empty space where the picture had been. 'Did you move it?'

'No, I didn't,' snapped Kate. 'And Eddie and Timmy can't reach up that high, not even standing on a stool.'

'Then who . . . ?'

Kate gave a long, shuddering breath. 'Just pretend everything's normal. We go back downstairs and finish our dinner. I'll tell Chloe that I didn't take it down because I didn't like it; I'll think of an excuse. Then we talk.' She caught hold of his arm. 'I know you must have, but did you lock up properly when you went out today?'

Trying not to feel hurt by the accusation, Tom said, 'Because of the situation, I double-checked every door and window, even though we do have two of Lincolnshire's finest watching this place like hawks.'

She squeezed his arm. 'I'm sorry, but I had to ask. It's one of the downsides of being a copper.'

Luckily, Chloe was easily placated when Kate told her she'd completely forgotten that she had taken it down to show Auntie Gerry, who had liked it so much that she had put it up on her office wall at work. The little girl cheered up immediately and tucked into her food.

Tom, on the other hand, had lost all appetite. Having quickly ruled out every other possible reason for the picture's disappearance, he was left with one. And that one was deeply troubling.

Table cleared and dishwasher loaded, the children went to watch a cartoon on the television, leaving Tom and Kate alone to talk. They faced each other across the kitchen table, neither of them knowing how to begin. Their silence was interrupted by the ringing of her mobile phone. Private number.

She stared at it, her blue eyes hard as steel.

'If it's him,' she hissed, 'get out to that car and tell them to ask for a "last number" trace to my mobile.' She exhaled, accepted the call and pressed the loudspeaker button.

The voice filled the room. 'Kaa-tie, Kaa-tie.'

Tom froze for a moment before leaping to his feet and racing out of the room.

CHAPTER TEN

'Who are you? What do you want with me?' Kate tried to keep her cool. The longer she could keep him on the phone, the better chance they had of a trace.

'Oh, Kate, really. You know who I am. As to the second question, you wouldn't want to know the answer.'

'I *know* you?' She could hear the shock in her own voice and cursed herself for not staying calm.

'Oh yes, you know me all right.' He gave an odd little laugh, almost a titter. 'But more of that later. I rang to say that I love little Chloe's painting of her mummy. So very cute.'

At the mention of her precious daughter's name, Kate lost it. 'You bastard . . .'

But he cut into the string of expletives. 'Shut up and think. Think how easy it was for me to take that picture. Don't you think I could just as easily take the child? Goodnight, Kate. Sleep well.'

The line went dead. Kate's heart was pounding. Her children? This was a whole new level. Or had he said it simply to put the fear of God in her? A threat to her was one thing, but her little ones?

She was still staring at her phone when Tom hurried back into the kitchen. 'They'll be in as soon as they get an answer,' he panted. 'So, what did he say?'

Kate told him. When she got to the bit about Chloe, his jaw tightened, his hand curled into a fist.

'If I ever get hold of that bastard, I swear I'll tear him limb from limb,' he cursed.

With a jerk, Kate came to herself. Suddenly she was all business. 'There are calls I have to make, Tom. The super needs to know, and Gerry; she'll need to inform the team. Can you wait to hear what the crew says regarding the phone trace? I don't hold out much hope though. More likely than not it was a burner phone and he's already ditched it.' She looked at him. 'Then we have to get the children away from here, as fast as we can.'

'Make your calls, and I'll deal with the guys outside. When we've done that, I'll tell you about the idea my parents had for what to do with the children.'

She rang Arun, who didn't sound all that surprised, though he was puzzled as to how he had managed to get into a secure property that had a police car watching it. He said he would call for a SOCO to go in, so she should make sure no one goes into the playroom. There might just be prints on the conference board, the doors or the windows.

She then phoned Gerry, who was horrified. She asked Kate if she was okay, and would she like her to come over. It was kind of her sergeant to suggest it, but Kate said no, they had to get the kids and the animals to safety. 'I trust this bastard about as far as I could spit. We'll even bring the duck and the tortoise indoors tonight, just in case. Oh, and that reminds me, can you ask Tony if Julie could possibly take Matilda, our little duck, while all this is going on? She's so good with birds. We'll have to move fast to get all this organised. Knowing that that evil bastard has been in the house is like a violation.'

'I'll get onto Tony immediately and call you back. I imagine you won't be coming in tomorrow,' said Gerry, 'you'll have your hands full at home.'

'I've let the super know, so after we've arranged everything, I'll come in and discuss the way forward with him. Are you okay to carry on with the investigation? I'll be back as soon as I can.'

Gerry told her not to worry, and just concentrate on keeping safe.

'I haven't had a chance to take it all in yet. He said I knew him. He meant it too. I'm so fucking angry!'

'You have every right to be,' her friend said. 'Don't forget, the team is right behind you. Ring us if there is anything we can do, and I mean anything. Day or night, okay? And I'll get back to you about the duck.'

Kate ended the call, and went to look for Tom, who was conferring with one of the officers from the observation car. When they saw her, the PC, a young lad called Dean, stepped forward, looking utterly miserable. He apologised profusely for having let the stalker get into the house. After a while she began to feel sorry for him, knowing the bollocking he was going to get from his sergeant.

'Hey, it might not even have happened on your shift, Dean. I was in the playroom with the children before dinner, and I didn't notice the picture had gone, so we have no idea when he got in — or how for that matter.'

'I just don't see how he did it, ma'am. We patrol the house and the garden regularly, and always at different times.

We checked the doors and windows, and we watch who's coming along the road.' Dean looked anxious. 'And I'm afraid the trace on your phone showed your caller used a burner, as I'm sure you suspected. Still, our tech guys are trying to pinpoint where the call came from.'

Kate nodded. 'I thought it would be, and I doubt the location will show anything. He's too clever for that.'

After Dean had returned to his crewmate, Kate said, 'Okay, Tom, tell me about your parents' idea for the children.'

'Mum and Dad said they are prepared to take them on a surprise "holiday". They'll decide where they'll be going after they get on the road. Dad has this new SUV, and there's plenty of room. He says they can take off with less than an hour's notice, if necessary.' He looked at her. 'I know your parents said they'd take them too, but they live too close to us. I think it'd be better if the kids were as far away as possible, what do you think?'

Kate stared at him, aghast. She had never yet been separated from her children, and the thought of summarily despatching them into the unknown made her want to weep. Then she recalled that voice telling her how easy it would be to snatch Chloe. 'As long as they let us know they are safe — every day without fail.'

'I'll clear it with their schools first thing in the morning,' Tom said. 'And in case our clever sodding stalker can hack phones, I'll make sure that when they ring, they never give a location.'

'So, when do we go ahead with this?' she asked, dreading the answer.

'First thing in the morning?'

She nodded, relieved. 'I thought you were going to say tonight, but we are here with them, and we can take turns to keep watch. And as that phone call was a definite threat, the super might even talk uniform into doubling the crews outside, then one can watch the back of the house.'

Gerry rang. 'Duck has a hotel room booked at Julie's. Tony can collect this evening if that helps?'

'I owe you a hug for that,' Kate said. 'Matilda is one of the family, and extremely vulnerable if we have a loony wandering around in the garden. We have a carrying cage, and we'll sort out some food. Tell Tony we are really grateful, and he can come at whatever time suits him. Just give us an hour to get her food and stuff together.'

'Another thing,' said Gerry. 'Julie's sister boards cats. Julie says she always keeps a couple of spaces free for emergency bookings. She's only a couple of miles outside town, and she will contact her for you if you want. She says it's spotlessly clean and they would be safe and comfortable. Her sister, Anna, is as dotty about cats as Julie is about her ducks and chickens.'

'That sounds too good to be true. We were wondering what to do with the cats. Our local cattery is fully booked until the weekend, so that saves us a whole lot of ringing around.'

'I'll get her number and her address from Julie, and text it to you.'

'You are a real lifesaver, Gerry. Thank you.' She ended the call, which Tom had been listening to on loudspeaker. 'Good friends mean a lot at a time like this, don't they?'

'You can say that again, babe.' He turned to go and then stopped. 'Um, how do we go about telling the children where the animals are going, and why they are being whisked off, in term time, with their grandparents?'

'Good point, especially as Eddie loves school so much.' Kate scratched her neck. 'Shit, that's a tricky one. We don't want any tantrums. Go get the duck, and I'll have a think about that one while I wait for Arun to ring back.'

Two minutes later she received a WhatsApp message with the contact details and address of the cat hotel. Rather than do it when the children were around, she rang immediately, and in a few minutes, both the cats were booked in for the following morning. She stood for a moment, pondering what to tell the kids. Then she came to a decision. As long as Tom agreed, it would be the truth, but a very diluted version.

Tom returned from packing Matilda's bags for her holiday. He had reached the same conclusion. 'We'll need to be tactful. We mustn't scare them, especially Chloe, but at the same time they have to appreciate that it's serious, and they must do what Gran and Grandad tell them.' It wouldn't be easy. Timmy was particularly astute and could well sense that something was going on. Nevertheless, they had to give them some explanation. Not to do so wouldn't be fair.

They were just formulating their story when Arun rang back. He said he had put in a request for a safe house but had been refused. Apparently, the situation was not deemed sufficiently life-threatening. He had more or less expected this response but it still made him angry. Kate told him what they had planned for the children, and he sounded pleased — and relieved. There would be two crews, he said, for tonight, and the following morning. His voice grew sombre. 'We managed to obtain an approximate location for the phone used for his last call. It was local, right here in town. But that's all we have, and as we all know, the phone will have been trashed by now, or the SIM removed. But it means he's right here, among us.'

'He was right here all right. Right in our home,' muttered Kate, and shivered. 'I just pray we can get through this without having to move house. Things like this taint everything.'

'Hang on in there, Kate. We *will* get him.'

The conviction in his voice lifted her failing spirits. Yes, they would get him. They had to, for her children's sake.

CHAPTER ELEVEN

Concerned as she was for Kate and her family, Gerry's mother only made things worse. She went on and on about the irresponsibility of mothers who continued to work while they had children. She seemed to have forgotten that some women — Gerry for one — had no choice. She and Mike had shared Nathan's care, until he left her for another woman; now it was all down to her, including earning their keep. She didn't know what she would have done without her father.

For once, an exhausted Nathan, tired from walking the sea bank with his grandfather, had gone to bed early. Gerry had turned in too, ostensibly to read, but really to get away from her mother and take advantage of the peace to think about Kate's stalker.

She shared a room with her son, which wasn't the best of arrangements for either of them, but it was the only spare room in her parents' house. At least it had its own bathroom.

While Nathan slept, she sat up in bed compiling a list of people who had either manifested threatening behaviour, or had been a cause for concern in some other way. She considered each one in turn, and in some cases the people closest to them — friends, wives, husbands, and even parents. The father of one young tearaway, who'd been put inside for drug offences, became so angry he had to be restrained, spending several hours in custody while he cooled off.

After half an hour, she had a page full of crossed-out names. She could think of no one who fit the bill for Kate's stalker. She stared at the page; she was missing something. There had been an incident, she knew there had, that had given them all cause for considerable anxiety. What the hell was it? She came to the conclusion that her memory of it was so vague because she hadn't been directly involved, and had only heard about it.

She searched the recesses of her mind and, slowly, odd memories began to surface . . . She had been working six days on, three days off, and when she returned to the station after her off days, everyone was talking about something that had taken place in her absence. What was it? She glanced at her watch; it was almost ten. Not late exactly, but she didn't want to wake Nathan by making a call. Instead, she sent a message to Tony, hoping he wasn't crashed out in front of the TV.

After a couple of minutes she received a reply: *Have only one name on my list of weirdos, Sarge, and it ties in a treat. Craig Henshaw. He'll be my first job in the morning, don't you worry.*

Gerry wrote down the name, but it meant nothing to her. She sent another message: *Remind me, Tony. What was that case?*

His answer jolted her memory. Of course. *He was the uncle of a twelve-year-old girl who went missing. Name of Jessica Knowles. She was never found, and he was the number one suspect for her abduction. He started to haunt the police station, buttonholing the boss on every available opportunity, swearing he had nothing to do with her disappearance. Remember it now?*

She replied that she did, and thanked him. She set the alarm, put out her light and lay in the darkness, dredging up all she could remember about little Jessica Knowles.

It wasn't easy, as the case had not actually been theirs. The Knowles family lived over to the east of the county, way out of their patch. Craig Henshaw, the uncle, had lived close to Fenchester, and Kate and Tony had been asked to pick him up for questioning. That was how he would have latched onto her. For weeks, he wouldn't leave her alone, begging her to help him, protesting his innocence. He loved his niece like his own daughter, he said, swearing that he wouldn't ever hurt her, that he'd rather die than hurt a child. He became such a nuisance that he had to be officially warned off.

Unused to sleeping in a single bed, Gerry shifted about. She missed her bed. Her home. Pushing these thoughts aside, she turned her attention back to Craig Henshaw. Having had no dealings with him herself, she couldn't summon a picture of him to her mind. She had been out of the office a lot of that time, so their paths hadn't crossed. Tony would know, since, along with the boss, he'd been involved in questioning Henshaw.

Just as she was drifting off to sleep, another name jolted her awake. She switched the bedside light on, hastily scribbled it down and glanced over at her son. Nathan murmured something, but didn't wake.

Sleep banished for the night, Gerry lay going through her memories of Jude Comfrey. He had first come to their notice after having witnessed a fatal hit-and-run, and Gerry had immediately found him intensely disturbing. It was mostly his eyes, she remembered, which had the hard, penetrating gaze of a bird of prey. Most unsettling of all was the way he had fastened that gaze on Kate Carter . . .

* * *

By eleven the following morning, Kate and Tom were alone in a silent house. Empty of children and animals, it seemed bigger somehow. It was quite intimidating. Tom almost tiptoed around when he made tea.

Kate went upstairs, made the children's beds and tidied up. After the initial shock, Tom had persuaded them that they were setting off on a big adventure. The logistics had been complicated; Tom's parents couldn't just pick them up in case they were seen. In the end, the children had been dressed for school and driven off at their usual time. Then, when he was nearly at the first school, Tom had doubled back and driven to his parents' house.

The dogs had been collected, and Kate had driven the cats to their holiday home. Only Brian remained. He was now ensconced in the conservatory, in an indoor pen built for him by Tom, which gave him plenty of space to stretch his stocky little legs.

Back downstairs, Kate was somewhat surprised to find Tom vacuuming the kitchen.

'Just keeping busy, sweetheart,' he said sheepishly, turning it off. 'And making some noise. When I'm working and trying to concentrate, I long for a bit of quiet. Now, on the other hand . . .'

He was right. It was far too quiet. No children, no animals. It seemed like the life had gone out of their home. 'That bastard,' Kate said. 'Just a few small acts, and he has turned our world upside down. We don't even know yet who we're dealing with.'

'A fucking nutter, that's who,' muttered Tom. 'How the hell did he get in here, that's what I want to know. Even your SOCO couldn't work it out.'

True, but the fact remained that he had got in. Since she had nothing better to do, maybe she should take a look for herself. 'Come on, Tom, let's put your mind at rest. We'll take a walk around and see if we can work it out. Unless he can walk through walls, there must be something everyone's missed.'

'So, where do we start?' Tom said.

'Suppose we start at the bottom and work our way up. We'll go through every room, checking all the doors, every window. Don't forget, there's the attic too.'

Their house wasn't new. Built in the 1940s, it had undergone a number of additions, alterations and improvements over the course of its life. The only modern renovation was the extension of the carport and the construction of a big room over it.

They had been searching for almost an hour when, just as Kate was starting to believe that he could indeed walk through walls, she gave a cry of satisfaction. 'So that's how he did it.'

They were in what had once been a pantry before the kitchen was extended. They used it now as a place to store items that weren't often used. She pointed to the window frame. 'This is the only room where the windows haven't been replaced. The window is shut, but look at the glass.'

Tom shrugged. 'It could do with a clean.'

Kate laughed. 'Don't you dare! You'll lose all our evidence. Those dirty marks, which are on the outside by the way, are sucker marks. He lifted out the pane and replaced it afterwards. Well, he certainly knew what he was doing; that's the work of a skilled house-breaker.'

'And he wouldn't be seen from the front or the side of the house,' added Tom. 'There are trees and shrubs close to that window, and the passageway round that side is blocked off at the end by the fence.' He turned and looked at her. 'How come your guys missed it?'

Kate was ahead of him. 'We were just lucky. The old pantry doesn't get much sun, and our lads checked much later in the day. I only saw it because the sun was on it so the sucker marks showed up.' She exhaled. 'Whew. This makes me feel a lot better. At least now I know he isn't a ghost. I'll ring Arun and ask if he can get a SOCO to come and dust the outside of that windowpane.'

She didn't believe they'd find anything, but it had to be done, and at least it would pass a bit more time. It was not yet twelve, and her appointment with Arun at the police station was for two thirty. Meanwhile, Kate kept seeing those forty-fives and wondering what they could mean. Stalker or no stalker, she had two murders to solve, and apart from wrecking her home life, he was creating havoc with her work.

* * *

Gerry, Tony and Luke were all in early that morning to discuss possible candidates for their DI's stalker. They had decided to keep what they were doing between themselves for now. Trevor was a nice enough guy, but he hadn't been with the team long.

Luke, who had also come across Craig Henshaw, agreed with Tony that the man was a likely suspect, particularly given the way he had hounded the boss.

That being the case, Gerry left her colleagues to concentrate on Henshaw, while she pursued Jude Comfrey. What she really wanted to know was his current whereabouts.

By the time they were due to start their "official" day's work, they had gathered a considerable amount of information. It was already starting to look as though Craig Henshaw was out of the picture. Their enquiries had revealed that he had moved away from the Fens, and was now living in Nottingham. Apparently, things had become too hot for him in Fenchester, following the case of his missing niece. He had been proved innocent, but mud sticks. Of course, there was always a chance that he'd come back, but Luke had phoned his employer, who confirmed that he was still with them and hadn't been absent during the past two weeks.

That left Jude Comfrey. Gerry looked into the file of the hit-and-run, where his details were recorded as a witness, but he had disappeared. She could find no forwarding address. Furthermore, on skimming through the reports, she noticed a comment from uniform that had cast doubt on the veracity of his statement. It hadn't registered as a cause for concern, but nevertheless, it bothered Gerry. She really needed to talk to the boss. Kate had a memory like an elephant, and would clarify the matter in an instant. The trouble was, Kate wasn't here. Gerry glanced at the office clock. It was now midday. Oh well, she'd just have to wait a couple of hours until Kate came in to report to the superintendent.

Gerry heard someone call her name, and saw a civilian member of staff standing in the doorway, looking around.

'Over here,' she called.

'I'm told the DI is out today, and there's a package for her. It's been scanned and it's safe to open. And there's some post for her too. Shall I leave it on her desk?'

Gerry went over. 'It's okay, I'll take it. Thank you.'

She stared at the padded envelope, addressed to Kate in even capital letters, and frowned. She pulled her phone from her pocket and called Kate on her mobile. 'Boss, a padded envelope has just arrived addressed to you, and I'm a bit worried about it.'

Saying she wasn't expecting anything, Kate told her to open it. Gerry rang off, slipped on a pair of nitrile gloves and opened the envelope with a paper knife. Slowly, she withdrew the contents, and gasped. In her hand, she held a folded sheet of paper — and an old pop record.

'Tony! Luke! Trevor!' she yelled. 'Over here, now!'

It was another forty-five, this time bearing a navy-blue Decca label. Once more, the centre was missing.

The four detectives stared down at it.

'What the fuck is this all about?' Luke said.

'Let me read the note,' said Gerry, opening up the folded sheet of paper.

Four words, written in the same uniform capital letters as the envelope, thereby rendering it useless to a handwriting expert: *ONE MORE TO DIE.*

'Another death?' breathed Tony.

'How else can we read it?' Trevor said glumly.

Gerry picked up her phone. 'This can't wait till the boss comes in; she needs to know about it right now.'

As she expected, Kate said, 'I'm on my way.'

She arrived twenty-five minutes later, looked at the record and the note and said nothing for several seconds. Then, 'Time for a campfire. My office.'

As the others moved away, Gerry touched her arm. 'Can I talk to you for a minute when we're finished? I know you're seeing Arun, but I really need your take on something.'

Kate raised an eyebrow. 'Murderers, or stalkers?'

'Your stalker.'

'Then we'll talk as soon as I've finished, okay?' Turning to go, she muttered, 'This guy is doing my head in.'

Inside her office, Kate sat perched on the end of her desk, and addressed her team. 'I reckon we can all agree that our killer has made contact — or if not the killer, it's someone who is very much in the know about what's going on. Those records are the key to the whole thing, so what we need to work out now is what connects the victims.'

'What I don't quite understand is what he meant by that note,' Trevor said. 'Is there about to be a third death, or was he referring to another long-dead body?'

'My money's on a new killing,' said Tony flatly. 'Because unless he sends us a damned GPS location, we could be hunting until Doomsday for a grave.'

'That's my thinking as well,' agreed Kate. 'Unless, as you say, he tells us where to look, which I think is unlikely.' She frowned. 'Look, guys, I can't be here full time yet, but I'm very anxious that we hold onto this case. I do *not* want Smithson taking over.'

The look on Trevor's face said he'd rather wrestle starving tigers than see that happen.

'If you can hold it together for me until my stalker is identified and banged up in a cell, I'm sure we can solve this case. But right now, you need a plan for how to proceed.' She turned to Gerry. 'Any updates since yesterday?'

'Nothing, boss. We are currently trying to identify the woman. If we can do that, we can see if she has a connection to our other victim, Stephen Clarke — other than an old pop record.' Gerry nodded towards Tony. 'Tony and Luke are about to head out to the Clarke home in Fleet St Michael, to see if they can find any of Stephen's old friends. Someone might know if there was ever another friend, who went missing around two years ago.'

'That's good. And you and Trevor?' asked Kate.

'We're working on those pop records, boss. Since they were all released in 1964, that date must have something to do with it, but we don't have much to go on.'

'This one too?' Kate pointed to the record that had been sent to her today.

'Trevor checked, and it's definitely 1964,' Gerry said. 'So it has to mean something, we just haven't a sodding clue what.'

'You'll get there,' Kate said. 'And don't forget to consider that all these records came from a jukebox. It might be relevant.' She slid off the desk. 'And, please, keep me updated. Even though my family and I are going through a rough time at present, I'm still in charge of this case, and I'm there for you, okay? I'd better go and see Arun now, but I'll pop in before I head off.' As she made to leave, she turned to Gerry. 'Never worry about contacting me. If I can't respond at once, I'll get back to you, I promise. Carry on trying to identify that dead woman and get that pop record to Cold Colin.' She smiled. 'Remarkably, he's being very helpful, and even more astoundingly, he knows a whole lot about 1960s pop records, so use him.'

Gerry had a sneaking suspicion that Cold Colin's remarkable helpfulness only extended as far as Kate, but she said she would do as suggested. She offered to take it herself so she could speak to the pathologist about it.

Back at her desk, Gerry told the others to grab some lunch before Tony and Luke headed off to Fleet St Michael.

She wasn't hungry but knew the folly of failing to eat. You never knew when the next opportunity would arise.

'Can I get you anything, Sarge?' asked Trevor. 'I'm going to nip across to the bakers for a sandwich and a doughnut.'

She accepted his offer, chose a tuna mayo sandwich, and went back to her computer.

Aware that the murders must take precedence, Jude Comfrey still haunted her. The murder cases would run a great deal more smoothly if their boss was back and firing on all cylinders. Of course, for that to happen, they needed to deal with her stalker. As far as Gerry was concerned, it was a no-brainer. The killer must be found, but the stalker came first. Even though Arun had told them not to bother Kate about it for fear of making things worse, Gerry knew how her boss's mind worked. If she knew her team were working in the background, she would be grateful for their efforts. Which was why she needed to talk to her about Jude Comfrey.

As she waited for her lunch, and for Kate to return, she couldn't shake off her conviction that Comfrey could be the stalker. She had no basis for it, but the looks he gave Kate would not leave her mind.

CHAPTER TWELVE

As Barney was washing up after his lunch, he heard someone knock at his door. He was expecting no one, and as Arthur and Lottie were his only friends in the house, he fully expected it to be one of them.

When he found Miss Enid Houghton standing outside, his jaw dropped. Hastily, he closed his mouth. 'Er, can I help you?'

'May I come in?' she asked rather formally.

'Oh, well, of course,' he stammered, standing aside, thanking heaven he had tidied up earlier. He pointed to the one old chair and asked if she would like to sit down.

For a moment or two the old lady stood looking around, seemingly taking stock of the tiny flat.

Barney's first thought was that she was checking to see if he was taking care of the place, until he saw her eyes linger on the damp patches over the window, and the mould that was clinging to the frame.

After a while, she sighed. 'Oh dear, it's worse than I thought.' She turned to the chair and seated herself, back straight, and regarded him. 'I owe you an apology. My friends the Montgomerys told me about the state of this room, and I now realise that I should have taken more care before I let it.'

There was really no need to apologise, Barney stuttered. It was an old house, and the costs of its upkeep must be horrendous.

Miss Houghton waved this aside. 'No. It is not right, and that's an end to it. Now, let's get on to how we can resolve it. Perhaps you would feel less uncomfortable if you sat too, young man.'

Barney obediently lowered himself onto the lumpy old sofa and regarded her with some trepidation. Was this going to be good news?

'Arthur Montgomery has put a suggestion to me, Mr Capstick, and I'd like a few assurances from you before we discuss the finer points of his proposal.'

Her piercing gaze rested on him while he nodded furiously. 'Of course, Miss Houghton.'

'He has suggested that you move into the vacant room on the ground floor. In return, you will spend time in the garden. I would like your assurance that I can rely on you to work in the areas I designate, and make it presentable again. Well?'

'It would be a pleasure, really it would. It's such a wonderful place, and I'd—'

'Yes, yes, but would you, along with your regular paid work, be able to continuously put in enough hours to cover the deficit in the rent on the better flat?'

'I can, and I will.' In conversation with Enid Houghton, it seemed, less was more.

'Then I propose a three-month trial period, commencing from the date when you move into Flat One.'

Standing to leave, her eyes fell on some of the sketches he'd made of the garden. 'What is this?'

Barney stammered like a schoolboy caught doing wrong. 'I . . . well . . . I was trying to visualise Knighton House garden in its original state. It must have been so beautiful. The groundwork is still there, so in time—'

'Why did you place that wrought-iron armillary on a plinth at the bottom of the long lawn?' she said, pointing at one of the drawings.

'Because I felt it belonged there,' Barney said, now on firmer ground. 'I noticed the old sundial rusting away in a flower bed and remembered that there was an area that would have caught the sun for most of the day. I haven't found the plinth yet, but I'm sure it's around somewhere.'

'You were correct, Mr Capstick, that was where it always sat.' Miss Houghton regarded him with something approaching respect. 'It has long been my wish to restore this place to its former state, but the garden, well, it seemed a step too far.' She picked up another sketch, this one showing the folly. 'You have a good eye, Mr Capstick.'

He thanked her, saying he had always had an interest in garden design.

Almost reluctantly, Miss Houghton laid the drawing down on the table. 'If you can put your talent to work on my garden, Mr Capstick, I think we will get along very well. Mr Payne will be leaving in two weeks' time, possibly before then. As soon as the flat has been cleaned and made ready, you may move in.'

Closing the door behind her, Barney let slip a yell of delight. He was going to buy Arthur and Lottie the best bottle of sherry that he could find.

* * *

Kate left Arun's office greatly relieved. Unless anything untoward happened, the murder case would remain in her hands. He gave her the option to work from home, communicating with the team via Zoom or Teams. She wouldn't have access to police records, though Gerry and the others could always look them out for her. Alternatively, she could continue coming into work, in which case she would be afforded protection, but that left Tom alone in the house. Arun advised her to discuss it with Tom, warning her that if the situation went on too long he would have no choice but to hand over the murder enquiry.

Meanwhile, Kate had come up with another option, which she wanted to discuss with Tom before putting it to Arun. Close to the police station was a former warehouse that had been renovated and subdivided into studio spaces for creatives or other self-employed individuals, and small partitioned-off cubicles intended as offices, along with Wi-Fi. Tom could easily work from there while she was at the station, and they could travel to and fro together. That way, Tom wouldn't be left alone, peering out of the windows, alert to the slightest noise, and neither job would suffer. To her mind, it was by far the best option. She just hoped Tom would see it that way.

She found Gerry waiting for her at the bottom of the stairs, and ushered her into her office. Gerry took a seat and began to tell her of the team's out-of-hours efforts to identify the stalker.

'I thought it might give you a bit of a boost to know we're behind you. I hope I've not overstepped the mark.'

Kate could have hugged her sergeant. 'Not at all, I'm just very grateful.'

Waving her thanks aside, Gerry asked her what she thought about Jude Comfrey. 'I don't know if you remember him; he was a witness in a fatal hit-and-run a couple of years ago.'

It didn't take Kate long to recall him. 'I mostly remember that he gave you the heebie-jeebies when we interviewed him.'

'He did, but that's not all. If you recall, uniform expressed doubts about the veracity of his statement. There was a discrepancy somewhere, but I'm not sure what it was.'

Memories of the case came back to Kate. On a lonely road in the middle of nowhere, a young man walking home from work had been struck and killed by a motorist who failed to stop. Neither car nor driver had ever been located. The only witness, Comfrey, swore that it had been a deliberate act. According to him, the car had accelerated as it approached the man and had driven straight at him. 'As I recall, one of the local beat officers was certain that, from where he was standing, Comfrey couldn't possibly have seen all he said he had. The officer mentioned the poor visibility due to a seafret that had come in, meaning the lane would have been shrouded in mist. Comfrey agreed that there had been a fret but as fenland mists tend to do, it had lifted briefly at the time of the accident.'

'And the fact of the mist couldn't be proven one way or the other,' added Gerry. 'The mists do swirl around, they do lift and descend like that. But the officer continued to insist that Comfrey was lying. I can't recall what reason he gave.' She looked across to Kate. 'I mean, why would Comfrey lie? There was no one else anywhere near, and he rang us immediately — or so he says. There was nothing to lie about.'

Kate pictured Comfrey. She had disliked him from the outset, and he did indeed have very unusual eyes; his stare was quite off-putting. Other than that, he was to all appearances a conscientious member of the public. 'What's the problem with him, Gerry?' she asked.

Gerry hesitated. 'It sounds stupid, but I just have seriously bad vibes about that man. I was with you when you interviewed him, and I saw the way he looked at you. You left the room at one point, and his eyes didn't leave that door until you came back in. Now I remember him, I can't stop thinking about it. I keep seeing his eyes, and the way he looked at you.'

Kate hadn't picked up on any of what Gerry was saying, but that didn't mean she was mistaken. 'Hmm. Come to think of it, I was spending more time writing my report than actually looking at Comfrey. He wasn't a suspect who needed close observation. I did notice his eyes though. I wondered at the time what it was that made them so disturbing.'

'I don't know,' Gerry said. 'We've been going through all the men you've had dealings with who could have an unhealthy obsession with you, and Comfrey is the only one who really stands out.' She grinned sheepishly. 'Well, to be honest, boss, I've already started trying to find where he now lives. He moved not long after the incident.'

Having no better suggestions as to a suspect, Kate said, 'Then keep me updated on your findings, and thank you again for putting in extra hours to help me, Gerry. You know how much I appreciate it.'

'No sweat, boss. We want this freak locked up too, so we can have you back with us.'

Kate told Gerry about the office space in the old warehouse, which she agreed was the ideal solution. 'Not just because it would mean us having you back, but it should give Tom a bit of peace of mind knowing you are close by, and surrounded by a load of flat-foots with tasers and handcuffs.'

Kate stood up. 'Right. I'll get off home and see what he thinks. I just hope Tom agrees. I really need to be here, but I have to consider his feelings as well. As you can imagine, we're both pretty distraught right now, what with the children being off heaven knows where.'

Gerry squeezed her arm. 'It must be hell, Kate. There's not a moment goes by when I don't worry about Nathan, and the effect the split with Mike is having on him. That's nothing compared with what you are going through. But don't lose hope. We'll find this creep.'

Then Kate did hug her.

* * *

Having listened to Kate's suggestion in silence, Tom asked if he could think it over. It sounded eminently sensible, but for some reason, he was loath to leave the house. He wished he knew why. The place was a sodding mausoleum. So why did he feel such a strong need to stay put? Yes, it was their home, the place the children would come back to if something went wrong. If one of the dogs escaped, they would run here. But was he being a prat thinking this way? Kate's suggestion made perfect sense. She would be safe; after all, she was the one being threatened. Still, he procrastinated.

He went out into the garden to find a few cabbage leaves for Matilda, then remembered that she wasn't there, and found himself wandering about aimlessly. There was, of course, another reason for his reluctance to leave. If the stalker came back, he'd be here, waiting. And there was nothing he'd like more than getting the opportunity to knock the shit out of that man.

CHAPTER THIRTEEN

Colin Winter stared thoughtfully at the third pop record. 'Another hit from 1964.' He looked at DS Wilde. 'I'd say that's your connection, Sergeant, wouldn't you?'

'We'd come to that conclusion as well,' said Gerry. 'Plus the fact that they're all ex-jukebox records.'

'That may be relevant too, but it could mean several things,' said Colin. 'They're still easy to pick up on eBay or wherever, or they could have belonged to a single collector. Personally, I'd take the jukebox route.' The sergeant gave him an inquiring look. 'By that I mean find a place that still has a jukebox. I saw one not long ago that was advertised in the local paper. Some café in the style of an American diner was closing down, so they were selling it. There are still some around, so it might be worth a few enquiries.'

'We'll do that,' said the sergeant, 'and thank you for your help.'

As she turned to go, he said, 'Where is the DI, Sergeant? I had the impression she was very interested in these records, and I'd expected her to bring it in person.' At his words, DS Wilde appeared to hesitate. 'I hope there's nothing wrong?'

'She, er, has some personal problems, Mr Winter, and, um, may need to take some time off work.'

'Knowing how dedicated she is, it must be something serious then,' he said. Colin knew all about so-called personal problems, and what they could do to you *and* your career. 'Is there anything one can do to help?'

The sergeant appeared to be on the brink of speech, so he waited. 'Well, the fact is . . .' Then it all came tumbling out. 'You see, DI Carter has attracted a stalker. He has threatened her youngest child, and we have no idea who he is or why he's terrorising her and her family.'

For a moment, Colin was speechless. Finally, he said, 'When you speak to her next, please tell her if there is anything I can do to help, she must not hesitate to contact me.' He pointed to the record lying on his desk. 'Meanwhile, I'll do whatever I can to help you solve this, er, conundrum. Rest assured that I will deal immediately with any forensic information that comes my way.'

'Would that mean any forensic evidence pertaining to the stalker too?' she asked hopefully.

'That especially,' he said. 'I find such behaviour sickening. It's a terrifying thing for any woman to have to deal with, and I am truly sorry for DI Carter.'

When the sergeant had gone, looking quite taken aback, he stared down at the record, wishing his father were still around. His dad would have known what these records meant, or at least where to look to get some answers. But his father had died years ago, so it would be down to him to find them. It would mean opening a few old wounds — one of which had barely healed.

Needing to think, Colin took the unprecedented decision to leave early. He went to find Jimmy Flynn.

'If you wouldn't mind dealing with as much as you can, Jimmy, and reschedule the rest for tomorrow, I shall be off for the rest of the afternoon. Is that okay?'

Jimmy Flynn looked utterly flabbergasted. 'I, well, yes, of course, sir. No problem at all. Is, er, everything all right?'

'I have no idea, Jimmy,' said Colin. 'None whatsoever.'

* * *

Gerry sat in her car and shook her head in disbelief. What had she been thinking? She must be mad, blurting out the story of her DI's stalker like that, and to Cold Colin of all people! But he had seemed so genuinely concerned about Kate. Somehow, her boss had broken through his icy exterior and exposed the real human being inside.

What was it about Kate? She was beautiful, but so were many other women. Kate had something more. Whatever it was, it had attracted a stalker, *and* thawed out Cold Colin, the iceman himself.

She stiffened. Could the two admirers be one and the same person? No. Impossible. For a start, she couldn't see him creeping around Kate's house, removing a windowpane and slipping inside to steal a kid's picture. It was a ludicrous idea.

With another shake of the head, she started the car and headed back to the station. At least one good thing had come of her visit: they now had forensic help regarding the stalker, and they'd be first in the queue for their reports. She just hoped she hadn't made a terrible mistake in revealing too much to Colin Winter. She'd have to tell Kate, but maybe she wouldn't say anything to the others just yet.

* * *

By supper time, Tom had relented, and while they cobbled together a makeshift meal, he told her he'd go along with her idea. He still felt the urge to beat the hell out of the stalker but decided it was a natural thing to want under the circumstances. Kate came first.

'The setup there is very impressive,' Kate said, getting cutlery from the kitchen drawer. 'And as you do all your work on your laptop, you can just walk in and get on with it.'

'That's true, and it'll be better than pacing around here getting more and more wound up. Who knows, he might give up if he sees the place empty all day.' He didn't believe that for a second, but it was a nice thought.

'The biggest thing is that I have the team behind me,' said Kate. 'And not only in the murder investigation, they're also on the track of the stalker.'

'I'm surprised the neighbours haven't spotted him,' said Tom, breaking eggs into a bowl. 'They're all keeping their eyes peeled. Any news on that window yet?'

'It's too soon to get any results back,' said Kate. 'But I swear he's done this kind of thing before. Not necessarily stalking, but he knew exactly what he was doing with the windowpane. Hell, he even put it back so we wouldn't notice that it had been removed.' She sliced a tomato, sending the juice spurting across the table. 'I keep thinking about him saying that I know him. Did he mean it literally, or do I just know of him? I didn't recognise the voice.'

Despite the vigorously sliced tomato, Kate seemed more relaxed, now Tom had agreed to her idea about the workspace. He wasn't too excited about working away from home, but if it kept him close to her, he'd do it. Hopefully this awful time would soon be over and they could get back to normal life, surrounded with kids and animals once more.

'Oh, darling, I'm so terribly sorry.'

He looked up, fork in hand. 'Sorry for what?'

'I'm sure this is all to do with my job. It must be. Someone's out to make me pay for something I did to them, all because I'm a police officer. Thanks to my job, I've brought this down on you and the children.' Kate looked distraught. 'Sod it! Even the animals don't know which way is up right now.'

So much for being more relaxed. Tom went to her and held her in his arms. 'We've always known there was a risk involved. I think we've done brilliantly — well, you have. I mean, every day you deal with so much crap at the station, and then you come home and are a perfect mother to your kids. Not to mention a wonderful wife. We'll get through this.' Suddenly he stiffened. 'Oh hell, the tomatoes are burning.'

* * *

Gerry, Luke and Tony were back in the Old Oak, going over what they'd achieved so far. It wasn't much, as the murders were taking practically all of their time. 'I made a list of other possible candidates,' said Gerry, 'just in case my hunch is wrong. This time I picked out vengeful criminal types, though I can't see any of them being as controlled and devious as Kate's stalker.'

'Yeah,' said Luke. 'They wouldn't send chocolates; they'd torch her car or something.'

'The more I think about Jude Comfrey, the more I think you're right, Sarge,' said Tony. 'Even the timing works out. Comfrey witnesses that hit-and-run, sets eyes on the DI and becomes obsessed with her. Being clever, he decides to wait before he makes a move, do some homework.'

'It would take time to get information on a police officer, wouldn't it?' said Luke. 'Especially getting hold of her private phone number, and finding out about her family and how they roll.'

'It would also tie in with him saying she knows him. Okay, she only spoke with him two or three times, but she does know him,' said Gerry. 'Our problem is, where the hell is he now? He's somewhere in this vicinity, he made the call to Kate from the town, and he's obviously been watching her home for some time. But everything we have for him has his old address on it, and he left there months ago.'

'Most likely he's using a false name and renting somewhere in town, or he could even be staying in a cheap hotel,' said Tony.

'Probably. And there's no way we'll find him in bedsit land.' Gerry sighed.

'And we don't have the time or manpower to trawl round all the hotels and guest houses in the area,' added Tony. 'Not with two deaths and the threat of a third hanging over us.'

'Oh, by the way, I had a call just before we left,' added Luke. 'Craig Henshaw is a definite no-no. He has a rock-solid alibi for the day the note was left on the boss's car. So he's out of the equation.'

Gerry started to feel guilty. Glibly, she had assured Kate that she'd move heaven and earth to find this guy, and they were getting nowhere fast. It was all well and good having a possible suspect, but if he couldn't be found, it wasn't much use. She was drinking wine today, and was considering chancing a second glass when her phone rang.

'Hi, Kate. Is everything okay?' Her boss told her that Tom had agreed to her suggestion, and that she would be back at work the following morning. They all heaved a sigh of relief.

'That'll make life so much easier. And we'll be able to legitimately do some ferreting into her stalker if she is there,' said Tony enthusiastically. 'After all, the boss and her family can't go on living under this shadow. For heaven's sake, they even had to send their children away for fear of what this arsehole might do. It's horrible.'

'I have a feeling the super is going to shift matters up a gear,' said Gerry. 'After all, threatening her daughter was a serious crime. Did you hear that she was refused a safe house?'

The other two shook their heads.

'It doesn't surprise me,' muttered Luke. 'These days, criminals get treated with kid gloves and sod the poor coppers.'

Deciding to call it a day, they separated at the door of the pub. Things were about to get busy.

CHAPTER FOURTEEN

Colin stood outside the familiar old house, remarking to himself on how shabby it looked. Throughout his childhood it had always been scrupulously maintained. Built by a seafaring man with an appreciation for the eccentric, the family had called it the Gingerbread House because it looked like something from a fairy tale. In fact, it was a quite outstanding example of master carpentry and design, but it was by no means traditional. Possibly having seen various styles of architecture on his travels, the original owner had decided to apply some of them when he retired onto dry land.

The house, which belonged to his uncle, had a green tiled roof, the edges of which were bevelled and slightly rounded at the corners, so it appeared to be made of some soft material. Colin's uncle Fergus had told him and his sister that it was made of marzipan. It had any number of windows, big and small; tiny ones shaped like portholes, while others were mullioned, and some had wooden shutters. The gables were elaborately carved, the oak front door huge and solid, with a massive cast-iron knocker. Beside the door a ship's bell hung, engraved with the name *HMS Bridestone*. Bridestone was the name of the house.

Colin stood at the door, unable for a moment to bring himself to knock. The outcome of this visit had to be worth the anguish that just being here again was causing. Ignoring the rust-encrusted bell, he hammered on the door. After several minutes, he heard the shuffle of unsteady feet and took a shaky breath. He hadn't seen his uncle in fifteen years.

Fergus Winter opened the door, and almost recoiled in surprise. The two men stood looking at each other.

'Well, lad. I wondered if I'd ever see you again.' He stood aside for Colin to enter.

Inside, the house was unchanged. Colin paused for a moment by the wooden staircase, enthralled.

'Come through to the study, lad. I was about to pour myself a wee dram, how about it?'

Colin accepted the offer. A measure of Fergus's twelve-year-old malt might help calm his nerves. Although it was not in the slightest bit cold, there was a fire burning in the study. As far back as he could remember, there had always been a log fire in this room.

His uncle handed him a cut-glass tumbler and motioned to the leather high-backed armchairs on either side of the fireplace. Colin lowered himself into one, assailed by an image of himself, sitting on the hearthrug with his sister, listening to Fergus read them a story. If only, Colin thought, he could go back and undo the past. Perhaps his uncle wouldn't be a recluse, fading away in this make-believe house. As for himself, would he be someone other than the bitter, acid-tongued loner that he was now?

It was a superb whisky. It seemed the old fox hadn't lost his touch.

Studying him over the rim of his glass, Fergus said, 'As I can't see you ever forgiving her, I suppose you want something from me.'

Colin returned the stare. 'You're right, I won't forgive her. But . . .'

'Well?'

Colin's next words surprised even himself. 'The rage I feel is eating away at me, it's killing me. I don't know what to do.'

'Just learn to accept that the past is past, lad, and nothing you can do will change it. You can, on the other hand, stop it blighting your future. Eh?' Fergus spoke gently, as if Colin was still a little boy, grieving over the death of his pet dog.

'But how? Where do I start?'

'Maybe you've already started, laddie.' He raised his glass and drank. 'So, what do you want from me?'

Where to start? 'I want your help, Uncle. My job involves working with the police—'

'I know what you do, lad. I've followed your career. Given what you were like as a boy, I expect you are a very good pathologist.'

This was unexpected. Having steeled himself for a bitter and acrimonious encounter, he had found instead . . . well, kindness.

'But I don't see how I can help you,' Fergus said.

'It's a sensitive matter, Uncle. If I tell you, will you be able to keep it to yourself?'

Fergus gave him a withering look. 'Who d'you think I'm going to blab to? The only people I see are the postman and the doctor, and I only see them a couple of times a year. So go on. What's it all about then?'

'The fact is . . . it's about pop records.'

* * *

Without their three children and seven animals Kate and Tom were finding the silence in the house hard to bear. Even the phone call from Tom's parents hadn't alleviated it.

They did their best by busying themselves around the house. Kate was sorting toys when her phone rang. 'Tom!' she cried. 'I think it's him.'

At once, he was beside her. And it was him. 'Kaa-tie. Kaa-tie.'

She was about to yell at him when he said, 'Check your messages.' Then the line went dead.

'Christ! What is it this time?' she muttered, and opened the attachment.

It was an image, a single shot obviously taken with a phone camera. Tom's parents, loading three children into an SUV.

As she stared at the phone, it rang again.

'It's all right, Kate.' She heard him chuckle. 'You don't need to panic. I'm not interested in your kids; I never was. There's someone else who's piqued my interest. Can you guess who that might be?' He laughed.

'You can stop worrying. You'll get no more calls from me.' The line went silent. She held her breath, waiting. 'Next time, it'll be face to face. Goodnight, my love.'

* * *

In his childhood, the room Colin was now being shown into had been the third bedroom. Like all the rooms in Bridestone, it was fairly large, full not of beds, but stack upon stack of vinyl records. A shrine, or possibly a museum, dedicated to the music of the sixties.

'It's all here,' said Fergus in a hushed tone. 'Not just my own collection, but every one of your father's records, all his posters, collectibles. And then there's that.' He pointed.

'You kept it! I thought it had been dumped when the house was cleared out after his death.' Colin stared at the jukebox. 'I didn't know . . . I never thought that you'd have saved this.'

'I didn't only save it, I've renovated it too. It works better than it ever did. Sometimes I play a record and give the neighbours something to complain about.' Fergus chuckled. 'Miserable sods can never sleep through that.'

Colin went across and ran his hand over the gleaming red and gold machine. An original Rock-Ola Regis 1495, holding one hundred vinyl forty-fives, it had been his father's most treasured possession. Following his father's funeral, Colin had left, refusing to have any more to do with his family. Thus, he never learned what was in the will, and had assumed that the jukebox had been either sold as part of the estate, or dumped.

Lost in his memories, he hadn't heard Fergus speak. 'Sorry, Uncle. What were you saying?'

'You said you wanted to ask about records.'

They seated themselves on an old retro couch — another museum piece — and he told Fergus the story of the records discovered with two very different murder victims.

When he had finished, Fergus sat, apparently deep in thought. 'I've spent the past fifteen years building this collection, cataloguing every item and hunting down any that were missing. That means I've spoken to practically every collector, hobbyist and dealer in the country.'

This was more than Colin could have hoped for. He knew, of course, that Uncle Fergus was as keen on sixties music as his dad had been, but had never imagined him to be so fanatical a collector. It was probably what kept him alive.

'We — that is, the police and myself — want to discover where these came from.' From a pocket of his jacket, he produced a photo showing the records. 'Three 1964 chart-toppers, all from jukeboxes.' He hesitated, fearing his reclusive uncle's response. 'The thing is, the police wish to contact anyone in the area who possesses a jukebox, or has access to records from that year.'

'Hmm,' said Fergus, getting to his feet. 'I think we need another drink.'

Back in the study and having refused one himself, Colin watched Fergus pour a tumblerful, his hand shaking slightly. 'Uncle? What is it? You look quite pale.'

Fergus stared into his glass and sighed. 'I'm not sure, laddie. Can I ask the names of the victims the records were found with? Don't worry, it will go no further than this room.'

Colin told him they only knew the name of one of them. The old man made no move to write it down. Either he had a good memory for someone in his eighties, or he recognised it.

'Leave it with me, Colin. Give me your number, and I'll phone you. I have someone in mind that I can ask. I can't contact him tonight, but I might possibly — only possibly, mind — have an answer for you tomorrow.'

'We'd really appreciate any help you can give us. You see, there may be more deaths.'

Colin got up to leave. As he did so, his uncle laid a hand on his shoulder. 'Try to put the past behind you, lad. I know you hated me for refusing to speak out, but I know that if she had survived that crash, your mother would never have forgiven herself for causing your sister's death. She paid the price, Colin. Let her rest now. And try not to hate me. Let it go, before it destroys you.'

Colin walked back to his car. Suddenly, he realised that he was crying, but he had no idea who for; whether his tears were for Isla, his mother, or his uncle. Or maybe they were for himself.

* * *

Her hands around a glass of brandy, Julia Tennant leaned forward on the sofa, and regarded her dearest friend. That Sam Page was also her ex-husband was neither here nor there. He also happened to be an internationally respected professor of psychology, and a consultant to the Fenland Constabulary. Hence, she had no qualms about discussing her present dilemma; that of the dangerous stalker hounding DI Kate Carter.

With every act she described, Sam's expression grew darker. When she had finished, he drew in a long breath. 'Hmmm. Looks like she's attracted a bad 'un all right.'

'The worst,' said Julia. 'And there's more. Arun Desai texted me with his latest threat only half an hour ago.' She told Sam about the photo the stalker had sent, and what he'd said thereafter.

After he had digested this account of mounting harassment, Sam said, 'I would think he's someone she met some time ago, and given her job, it must have to do with an investigation. However, I don't think he's acting out of revenge. He sounds to me like a sexual predator, and a devious and patient one at that.' He regarded her seriously. 'This Kate Carter is in a great deal of danger. I do hope the powers that be are giving it the attention it deserves.'

'Arun Desai certainly is, but I'm not so sure about the higher-ups. He asked for a safe house for her and her family and had his request turned down.' She shook her head. 'I'm of the same opinion as you, Sam, and I fear for her life.'

'So, what is her situation at present? Is she at home? Is someone with her? Or, best case, has she taken leave and disappeared for a while?' asked Sam.

'According to Arun, her husband is with her when she's at home, and a crew are watching the house, but she's decided to carry on working. They have a murder investigation running, and she is loath to let it go.'

'That's not enough by a long chalk,' Sam said. 'Murder or no murder, she's exposing herself to risk. I'm pretty certain her pursuer will be pre-empting every move. He's studied that woman until he knows her inside out, and it's he who is pulling the strings. Don't forget, in his eyes, the husband is expendable. He's just an irritant standing between him and his prey. He wants Kate Carter for himself.'

Julia knew all this, but it made her shiver to hear Sam put it so succinctly. Somehow, she had to convince those senior officers to act, and protect Kate before it was too late.

CHAPTER FIFTEEN

The atmosphere in the morning meeting was one of relief mingled with anxiety. It was good to have their boss back, but the mounting threats to her cast a shadow over them all.

Gerry reported on the little they'd managed to uncover so far. Tony went on to present the results of the interviews they had held with the murder victim's friends. Both he and Luke believed these friends were holding back something from Stephen's past.

'Did any of them come across as being more nervous, or perhaps suggestible, than the others? If so, maybe you could go back and lean a little harder,' Kate suggested.

Tony and Luke glanced at each other. 'Yeah,' said Luke. 'There was one woman, name of—' he glanced at his tablet — 'Yvonne Burton. She was quite twitchy. I reckon we could have another word with her.'

'Then as soon as we've finished here, get back to Fleet St Michael. And don't be afraid to come down on her like a ton of bricks if you need to.' Kate grinned. 'Within reason, of course.'

'I've a feeling Cold Colin is going to come up with the goods,' Gerry said. 'Like you said, he knows more about those records than us, and I'm certain he'll try his best to help. I couldn't believe it when I went to see him; he was nothing like the man we've all come to know and, um, love. How did you manage to pull it off, boss?'

'Me? I didn't do a thing!' exclaimed Kate.

'Maybe, but it's you he wants to help.' Gerry grinned. 'I reckon you've charmed him, boss. And a bloody good thing too. Having him behind us could be a game changer — or speed things up anyway.'

Kate was about to answer when she noticed the superintendent standing in the doorway.

'Sorry to interrupt your meeting, but I just wanted to add a couple of things,' said Arun. 'It concerns your stalker, Kate. I am pleased to see you back, but please make sure that you go nowhere alone, and I mean nowhere.' He looked around at the team. 'And you detectives need to follow this to the letter. No excuses, not even suspected emergencies. Your DI is to have a police officer with her at all times. Is that clear?'

Having made this understood, Arun turned to Kate again. 'Since you can't go out alone to meet Tom for lunch, tell him to come here and have his with you. He'll worry if he doesn't see you. And, last thing, Julia Tennant is coming in this morning; she wants a quiet word with you. So come to my office in an hour's time.' On his way out, he paused and looked back. 'Thanks, everyone, and remember what I said. Keep your eyes open.'

'Okay,' Kate said. 'Tony and Luke, go and do your tough cop bit. Ring me if the woman comes up with anything of use. Trev, you and Gerry carry on with your efforts at identifying the woman in the barn. I'll be in my office with the door wide open, so you can all see that I haven't gone off alone somewhere. And, guys, I know the super means well, but let's not get paranoid. We need to deal with the two murder victims before we learn that there's a third.'

Gerry and the others assented, but reluctantly. None of them felt comfortable about the situation. Following the stalker's last call, the danger level had risen, and now Gerry doubted whether Kate should even be here. If it was up to her, she would have spirited Kate and her husband away and put them in some secret hiding place, a long way from here. She'd take their phones from them and give them burners so their location wouldn't be traced. Only then would Kate be safe, and they could continue their search for this bastard. Jude Comfrey — it *had* to be him. Why else disappear without trace?

A call from the mortuary interrupted her thoughts. Cold Colin sounded odd, almost frightened. 'Can you come here, DS Wilde? As soon as possible, if you wouldn't mind. There is someone here I want you to meet.'

Gerry said that of course she would come. 'The DI is at the station today. Would you like me to tell her?'

'I think that's a good idea, Sergeant,' Colin said, 'since it involves her.'

Gerry ran to Kate's office and told her. 'He sounded sort of, well, shocked. He didn't say what it's about, and I didn't want to waste time asking, but he wants us there pronto.'

Kate grabbed her jacket. 'Then let's go. I've still got an hour before my meeting with Julia.'

'Oh, I nearly forgot,' said Gerry. 'The super said we must have a uniformed officer with us whenever we go out. I'll get that organised and we can meet them in the car park.'

The additional delay obviously annoyed Kate, but to Gerry's relief, she didn't argue.

In minutes, they were in a car driven by a burly police constable who went by the name of Big Ted. It wasn't far to the mortuary, but Gerry spent the entire journey with her fists clenched and her jaw tight. Things were indeed hotting up, and fast.

* * *

Colin met them at the mortuary entrance and hustled them off to his office. Inside, they found an elderly man seated at Colin's desk. Colin introduced him as his uncle, Fergus Winter, who, as he put it, knew all there was to know about sixties culture, and owned an extensive collection of pop records from the decade.

Kate nodded. This was good news, wasn't it, so why did they look so grave?

'After I told him about your case, Uncle Fergus contacted a fellow collector of sixties records. From this man, he learned something so disturbing that he came in person to tell me about it. The story he was told explains exactly why those old pop records were found with your victims. Uncle?'

Kate leaned forward, holding her breath.

With a quick glance at Colin, Fergus cleared his throat. 'Years ago, there was this young man called Phillips — I forget his first name — who was heavily into sixties pop music. He was extremely well off — Daddy a successful businessman, posh manor house, fast cars, you know the kind. Well, he bought this jukebox, and set up a kind of club, or bar, in the cellar of his house. It was intended as a place to hang out in with his mates, but word got around, and soon it became the place to go on Saturday nights. He called it the Sixty-four Club.'

Kate threw a glance at Gerry, who raised an eyebrow.

'It didn't take long for problems to arise. He hadn't bothered to obtain a licence, so the kids started smuggling in their own booze, and then drugs. He was given a warning, and closed the place down, but after a while started up again, on a smaller scale, only opening on odd nights, the dates and times announced by word of mouth.' He coughed. 'Can I have a drink please, lad? My throat's parched.'

Stifling a smile at Cold Colin being called a lad, Kate waited on tenterhooks.

'There were a few wild boys,' Fergus continued, 'girls too, who started to frequent the place. Your victim, Stephen Clarke, was one of the bad 'uns. Not criminal like, but he was a bit of a rebel. Along with another lad, him and his girlfriend, who was just as bad as him, enjoyed getting the younger girls drunk so they could laugh at them. As far as I can tell, the Phillips lad didn't much like these goings on — he was really just a music fanatic, but he did turn a blind eye, even though some of the girls were obviously little more than school kids.'

'Your friend told you all this, did he?' Kate said.

'He and I used to find records for Phillips and sell them to him. He was from a much younger generation, but we all shared a passion for old vinyl. My friend had more to do with him than me, and Phillips used to confide in him — bit of a father figure, I suppose — but I did know about the Sixty-four Club.'

'I guess you're telling us all this because something bad happened,' Kate said.

'Aye, lass, it did.' He sighed. 'According to what my friend told me, one night, Stephen Clarke and his two friends slipped a drug into a young girl's drink. She went into a convulsion, and, before help could arrive, the poor girl died.' Fergus Winter shook his head. 'Now I'm told Stephen Clarke has been murdered, along with another woman, and my nephew says he fears there may be a third. You see, I know the name of your dead woman, and possibly that of the next victim.'

Beside her, Gerry already had her notebook out, her pen poised.

'Clarke's girlfriend was called Toni Shields, and his mate's name was Sean Raynor. That's all I can tell you, other than that Phillips is long gone. He went abroad not long after the girl's death. The house is empty, been on the market for years, though I'm willing to bet there's still an old jukebox in that cellar.'

A silence fell over the room. After a while, Kate said, 'Do you have any idea who killed Clarke, and possibly Shields, if we find that the body is hers?'

'Someone who cared for that dead girl. Stands to reason, lassie. Her name was — let me think. Mel, yes that's it, Melanie Dennis. She was nineteen, old enough to have had a serious boyfriend — or girlfriend maybe. Or her father, or a sibling. Trace the dead girl, and you'll have your murderer.' He rested his gaze on Kate. 'I don't mean to tell you how to do your job, but if I was you, I'd get a shift on and find Sean Raynor, before he turns into your third dead person with a calling card in the form of a 1964 pop record.'

* * *

As soon as they got back to the car, Kate rang Trevor and asked him to pull out the old case file. She also phoned Tony and told him to forget their interview with Yvonne, they had enough to go on for now.

'It never ceases to amaze me how just one chat with the right person can give us the very lead we're after,' Gerry said. 'It's all so random, isn't it, so dependent on making the right connection. Shall I start chasing up Toni Shields when we get back?'

'We'll have a swift meeting and divvy up the tasks,' Kate said. 'We have several leads to follow, and as Fergus rightly said, priority one is to find Sean Raynor.'

'Indeed it is, lassie,' said Gerry, in an atrocious Scottish accent.

Kate rolled her eyes. 'I nearly exploded when he called Colin "lad". And I couldn't believe my eyes when he scuttled off to get his uncle a glass of water. I'm really starting to see our Cold Colin in a new light. He's been pivotal to this entire investigation.'

A deep voice rang out from the front of the car. 'What? Our frosty pathologist? Are we talking about the same man?'

'The very same, Big Ted. But maybe don't spread it around, in case it's a temporary glitch in his brain cells,' Gerry said.

Good luck with that, thought Kate, knowing it would be all over the mess room within half an hour. Right now, however, she had more to think about than a bunch of gossipy men. If it was known that Clarke had administered that drug, why hadn't he been charged? And who was killing off the people thought to be responsible for the girl's death?

They arrived back in the investigation room with only ten minutes to spare before her meeting with Julia Tennant. She gathered the team in her office for a brief meeting. 'Gerry will fill you in on the details, and I'll be back as soon as I can. Trevor, would you get the office manager to run off copies of the old case file for each of you? Depending on what we find there, we'll prioritise what needs to be done. Gerry, alert uniform that we need an Attention Drawn issued for a Sean Raynor. He's in grave danger if he's not already dead. Raynor is victim number three.'

CHAPTER SIXTEEN

Barney was up early, and was ready to go by eight a.m. He had decided to start by drawing up a plan of the first two areas to be tackled as soon as he was fit to work. He had agreed with Enid Houghton to begin with the grassy stretch of former lawn below her apartment, so at least she would have that to wake up to each morning. It was just a pity that there was no money to buy new plants; he could see it now, ablaze with June colour. Still, a number of the perennials had survived, and with some heavy pruning might be coaxed back to life. First, he needed to tame the jungle — cut everything back, take out the dead parts, and mow the grass. That done, he could turn his attention to the part that really interested him, layout and design.

Barney downed the last of his coffee, picked up his notebook and made his way downstairs. His back was already much less painful, and he looked forward to getting down to some hard work again.

He paused on the landing and looked out of the window. Below, on the drive, was a car with an open boot, into which a man was loading assorted pieces of luggage.

Barney smiled to himself. So, Ricketts was moving out today. Good news indeed, as he worked for the same company as Eric Payne, the tenant of the flat he was going to move into. Maybe Payne would be leaving today as well. Happy days!

Outside, he headed for the patch of grass he intended to mow, and was slightly disappointed to see Eric Payne walking over to his car, empty-handed. Oh well, it wouldn't be long — less than two weeks — before that ground-floor flat became his.

It was a bright, sunny morning with a distinct nip in the air. He was impatient for the long daylight hours of summer to arrive. Meanwhile, there was a lot he could accomplish, in order to be ready when spring did come.

He spent half an hour or so making notes of the jobs that needed to be done. The small edging wall to one of the flowerbeds had collapsed and would have to be rebuilt, along with resurrecting the two lovely old wrought-iron obelisks whose climbing roses would have to be pruned back hard.

Barney turned his attention to the trellises on the walls of the house and sighed. They needed replacing, but he couldn't see Miss Houghton affording new ones. He'd just have to "make do and mend", as his mum used to say. He walked across to take stock of what might be needed. A few bits of wood wouldn't break the bank; his mate Simon, who was a chippie, might have some to spare.

It wasn't until he was close to the house that he realised that the two sets of windows on the far side of the old property belonged to his new flat. It was just to the right of them that the trelliswork started. Suddenly, he was overtaken by an urge to take a look at his new home.

Barney hesitated. He wasn't a nosy person, but it wouldn't do any harm just to see. The flat would be his shortly, Eric Payne had gone to work, so why not have a quick peek?

Glancing around, he stepped into the overgrown flowerbed beneath the windows and, pretending to check the trellis, peered into the room.

From what he could see, the place was certainly pretty spartan. He pressed his nose to the glass and squinted. And was rewarded by the sight of a large suitcase, partly packed, sitting open on the sofa, a pile of folded clothes next to it. With a gleeful smile, he turned his gaze onto the room itself. It wasn't huge, but it was much bigger than his, and the furniture looked quite decent. He saw oak panelling, and — joy of joys — a fireplace. Barney saw himself sitting by a log fire on a winter's evening, reading or just staring into the flames.

Barney drew back. Dare he take a look at the bedroom? The window was only a few paces along, and no one was around to see him.

When he reached it, he saw that the curtains were pulled. Bugger. He would have liked to see the place where he'd be spending his nights.

He turned to make his way back to the grass when he saw a large piece of concrete in the far corner of the bed, and realised it was part of the plinth that held the armillary. Excellent. If he could just find the rest and get that old sundial spruced up, Miss Houghton would have her centrepiece back.

He edged towards it along the bed, pulling aside the tendrils of the rampant bramble. He glanced again at the bedroom window and noticed that the curtain hadn't been drawn tight. Glancing around, he bent down and peered in. Like the living room, it was almost bare of anything but the furniture — a double bed and a chest of drawers. If there was a wardrobe, it was out of sight.

Suddenly, Barney felt ashamed of himself. He was behaving like a voyeur. A bedroom was a private place. He stepped away and continued towards the piece of concrete, which turned out to be only part of the armillary's base. He'd have to look further for the rest.

* * *

Kate's meeting with Julia Tennant left her feeling jittery. She phoned Tom immediately and told him that Julia had interceded on her behalf, with the result that a safe house had been made available to her. She asked him to come straight to the station; she'd send out for sandwiches and they'd talk it over. Moving into a safe house was the last thing she wanted to do, but Julia had made it clear that Tom could also be in danger. Kate, she said, had more or less dumped him in a room full of strangers. This was not going as she had planned, particularly because they'd just had a major breakthrough in the case. She was desperate not to have to leave it at this crucial stage, but how could she not, with her husband alone and unprotected. It seemed she had only the rest of today to get some answers before the super pulled the plug on her.

Determined not to waste a moment, she strode into the outer office. 'Okay, everyone. Updates, please!'

'Sean Raynor is missing,' Tony said. 'He didn't come home last night. He's a bit of a fly-by-night, apparently, so his partner wasn't all that worried, but when he still hadn't returned by the morning, she started to worry that something had happened to him.'

'She's not the only one,' added Gerry. 'I've a horrible feeling we are too late for Sean.' She handed Kate a print-out. 'This is a statement given by Toni Shields's father. It basically says she was always a troublesome child, who was in the habit of suddenly taking off. According to this, there were times when he didn't even hear from her for weeks on end, then she'd stroll in, without a word of explanation. Matters finally came to a head, culminating in a huge row, after which she stormed out, and he's seen nothing of her since. He assumed she had chosen to stay away, and had never considered the notion that something could have happened to her.'

'Has he been prepared for the worst?' asked Kate.

'Yes, and from the way he described her, and from a photo he gave us, it's almost certainly her,' Gerry said. 'Poor bloke wants to see her, and I don't think he should, not the state she's in.'

'Some people need to see their loved one, Gerry, no matter how bad they may look. It provides them with closure. They can give up waiting and try to pick up the pieces of their lives. Even the sight of a few bones — if they are indisputably those of the loved one — will allow them to start the grieving process. Anyway, we'll cross that bridge when we have confirmation from forensics.'

'I've already sent Colin a copy, he's working on it as we speak.'

'Good. But not so good where Sean Raynor's concerned.'

'No,' said Gerry. 'And there's been no response to the attention drawn. No one's seen him since yesterday afternoon when he left work. His car hasn't been traced either.' She grimaced. 'What's the betting he's nose-down in a ditch with a pop record in the glove compartment.'

Kate moved on. 'Anyone had a chance to look at the old case file yet?'

'I have, boss,' said Trevor. 'The verdict was death by misadventure. In other words it was never proved that Clarke, or either of his friends, or anyone else for that matter, administered the drug that killed her. It was suggested that she took the drug on her own initiative, since she was apparently not averse to experimenting with different sorts of high. A tablet wrapped in foil was found in her bag, which forensics identified as a variant of Ecstasy, mixed with an amphetamine. If what Fergus Winter said is true, then I reckon everyone involved in the Sixty-four Club, possibly even Phillips himself, closed ranks to protect themselves. Clarke wasn't even a suspect, that's why he doesn't appear in the record. The conclusion was that nineteen-year-old Mel Dennis had taken a drug while unaware that she was seriously allergic to it, so her subsequent death was deemed a misadventure.'

'But someone believed otherwise,' murmured Luke. 'And is now dishing out death sentences. And I've finally fathomed out the reason for the long gap between the first death — Toni Shields — and that of Stephen Clarke.' He read from his tablet: 'At around the same time as Toni went missing, Clarke and Raynor took a year out and went backpacking in various very remote places. They would have been hard to find. In my opinion, they suspected that Toni's disappearance was connected to Mel's death, and made themselves scarce.'

Kate nodded. 'That would account for the gap all right, but our killer hung about, didn't he? He wasn't going to give up; he really wanted those young men to pay for what they did.' She looked at her team. 'I reckon he's a local, and kept his ear to the ground regarding Clarke's travels. So, the next step is to talk to Mel Dennis's parents and her old friends — not the ones she partied with, but her school friends and besties. People who knew the real Mel. We need to know if she had a boyfriend, or whether a relative or close family friend appeared dissatisfied with the verdict. Gerry, you know the score and what to ask, so I'll leave that with you.'

'Sure. But we have a problem. While I was talking to Colin about getting a positive ID for Toni Shields, I asked him for the name and contact details of his uncle Fergus's record-collector friend. Unfortunately, he is very ill, on borrowed time, apparently, which is why Fergus called on him in person. He was able to manage a few words with an old friend, but he isn't strong enough to make a formal statement to the police.'

Kate winced. 'Even so, we must corroborate what Fergus told us, or it will be dismissed as hearsay. I wonder if you could go with Fergus to see him? We won't need any more from him than a few words of confirmation.'

'That's just what I was thinking,' said Gerry. 'In fact I've already asked Colin to put it to Fergus. He'll ring me back as soon as he gets an answer.'

Kate glanced at her watch, wondering why it was taking Tom so long to get to the station.

* * *

Having been warned by his doctor that he must be more active or his health would suffer, Fred Cartwright adopted a little spaniel from a rescue home and walked him twice a day. Today, much to Poppy's disgust, he had had to wait for a delivery, and it was almost lunchtime by the time he set out. In order to make it up to the dog, he decided to take a longer route through a wildlife reserve and up a bank which gave a view across a small reservoir. The spaniel always became terribly excited when she saw the ducks, and, small as she was, it took all his strength to prevent her dashing into the water.

'Nearly there, kid,' he said to the dog as they ascended the bank. 'What'll we find today, eh? Mallards? Plovers? Or something more exotic? There was a white egret last time we came, wasn't there?'

Poppy pulled ahead; she didn't care what birds they saw.

Fred always looked forward to the moment when he reached the top of the slope and looked out over the water. They were in luck today. There were several different species of wildfowl scattered across the reservoir. He made for the bird hide, so that he might sit and watch them through his binoculars. Poppy was fine with that as long as she had a treat or two to keep her occupied.

On reaching the hide, he was surprised to find it occupied — normally he had it to himself. On one of the benches, a man sat, slouched forward, head down. He appeared to be asleep.

'Sorry, mate, didn't mean to disturb you.' Turning to go, Fred heard Poppy growl. Poppy never growled.

The man hadn't stirred. Fred took a tentative step forward. And saw the blood.

* * *

Colin and Jimmy Flynn gently eased the man's body off the wooden bench and laid him in an open body bag on the floor of the hide.

'Same method as with Clarke, isn't it?' said Jimmy Flynn, eyeing the puncture wound in the man's neck.

'Identical,' murmured Colin. 'And if we needed any more proof that it's the same killer, I reckon this clinches the deal.' The black vinyl disc that the man must have been holding was covered in blood. 'Surprise, surprise, the date is 1964. It seems we have just made the acquaintance of Sean Raynor, but rather too late to ask him who was out to get him.'

He put the record in an evidence bag and turned to his assistant. 'Get some uniforms to help you carry him to the hearse. As soon as the SOCOs have finished here, get yourself back to the lab while I have a word with the detectives. I won't be long.'

Outside, he found DS Gerry Wilde talking to a man with a small spaniel at his side. Of course, the ubiquitous dog walker. How many bodies, he wondered, had been discovered by dog walkers out for a happy ramble.

Though shaken, the man was saying how glad he was that it was he who had discovered the body. Groups of schoolchildren were often brought here to look at the birdlife, and the thought of children . . . It was just too horrible. When he'd finally run out of exclamations, Gerry took his details and told him he was free to go. As soon as he was out of earshot, she turned to Colin. 'Sean Raynor?'

He held up the evidence bag. '1964. Sergeant Wilde, I guess this means our killer has completed his task.'

'Too late.'

'Two very sad words, Sergeant. Empty ones, I'm afraid. I also wanted to tell you that my uncle is willing to take you to meet his friend. He asks only that you be so good as to go alone. Please, no horde of uniforms, and keep it as brief as possible.'

'Thank you, and I won't need to stay long. Since it was his friend who had the connection with Phillips, we just need confirmation that what your uncle told us is true. I also need a few details about Phillips himself, since we might need to interview him. But I won't subject a sick man to a grilling.'

'Then if I give you my uncle's address, I suggest you go now. Uncle Fergus doesn't like going out in the dark anymore, and his friend goes to bed very early.' He took out a notepad and scribbled down the address.

'There's not a lot more to do here. I'll let Luke tie up the loose ends, and once the body has gone, the rest will be down to uniform and your SOCOs.' She pulled out her mobile. 'I'll just ring the boss and tell her where I'm going.'

'Good,' Colin said. 'I'll call Uncle Fergus and tell him to get ready for an outing with a policewoman.'

CHAPTER SEVENTEEN

Just as Kate was about to send a squad car to fetch him, Tom walked in. He had left his charger on his desk and had to go back for it. When he got there, he found that someone had kindly locked it in a cupboard, and the keyholder couldn't be found.

After a quick sandwich in her office, Kate sorted out a spare workstation for Tom, saying he was to work from there, where she could see him, and then returned to the investigation.

She was now waiting to hear from Gerry concerning the dead man found in the bird hide. There was no doubt in her mind that he would turn out to be Sean Raynor. Too late to save him, they now knew in which direction to look for the killer. It had to be someone close to Mel Dennis, the dead girl.

When Gerry rang and told her that Colin had found a 1964 record with the victim, Kate's suspicions were confirmed.

'If it's okay with you, boss,' said Gerry, 'I'm going to go and speak to Fergus Winter's friend. It will be another box ticked off. Apparently, the old guy is in poor health and can't have late callers.'

This was good. The more they could get sorted now the better. She ended the call and went over to Tony's desk. 'What have you lot managed to dig up on the dead girl, Mel Dennis?'

Tony stared at his screen. 'Quite a bit, actually. She certainly wasn't a tearaway, that's for sure. I've just spoken to a young woman called Ellie Pearson, who was a schoolfriend of hers. She says that Mel was a sweet girl — kind and considerate. Ellie insisted that there was no way Mel would have taken drugs, apparently; she was against them, and with good reason. We won't be speaking to her parents; they were both totalled in an RTC, caused by — guess what — a teenage driver high on alcohol and drugs.'

Kate frowned. 'So, she wouldn't have been experimenting with E then. But surely that came out at the inquest?'

'It says here that there were several close friends who all vouched for her,' Tony said, 'but there were even more from the Sixty-four Club. They said she was pretty wild, a real party animal. When I mentioned that to Ellie, she told me that was utter crap. She did admit, however, that Mel had fallen for a guy called Stephen, even though he already had a girlfriend, and she reckoned he was a bad influence on her.'

'Sounds like the old story of a nice kid falling in with the wrong people, doesn't it?' Kate said.

'Yeah, sadly it does,' said Tony. 'But wait, there's more. Ellie gave me some names of other old friends of Mel's, all of whom agreed with Ellie, but there was one who added a couple of interesting bits of information. Mel had had a boyfriend before she started hanging around with Stephen Clarke. He was about six years older than her, and he was well cut up when she died. His name is Carl Pennington. I haven't managed to track him down yet, but I'd say he's a priority, what d'you think?'

Kate nodded. 'Absolutely. Keep on with that, and perhaps get Trevor to help you. But you said a couple of things, what's the other?'

'When I was reading the coroner's report I noticed that Mel is short for Amelia, not Melanie as Fergus believed. Anyway, this old friend said that after her parents were killed, she went to stay with an aunt and uncle, but she was very close to her maternal grandmother . . .' He checked his screen. 'Enid Houghton. She lives on the fen, about eight miles from town. If anyone can tell us about Mel and the people who cared about her, it'll be her. Apparently, the old lady idolised her.'

Kate's eyes sparkled with excitement. 'Sounds like it's time to go cold calling. What do you reckon?'

Tony stood up. 'I'll arrange a crew to go with us — am I right in thinking you're coming too? I get the feeling you're determined not to be left behind this time.'

'Just be quick. I'm anxious to gather as much evidence as I can before I get thrown off this case and it's handed to Smithson.'

'Heaven forbid!' Kate turned to see Trevor looking utterly horrified. 'Anything but that.'

Kate smiled at him. 'Hold the fort here, Trev, and keep my husband supplied with coffee, all right? Try and trace this Carl Pennington too. If anything of importance comes up, ring me.'

Tom was listening to all this with a face that grew ever more gloomy. 'I suppose I couldn't come with you, could I? It's just that thinking of you out there while I'm stuck in here is agony.'

'Oh, sweetheart, I'm sorry but I can't risk it. If you were to get hurt, I'd be in serious trouble.'

She hated mixing her two lives like this. Tom should be at home, not sitting in a corner of her office. Though she didn't like to admit it, having him watching her was a constraint. Here at work she was someone completely different to the person she was at home. It was yet another reason to curse the bastard who was behind all this.

* * *

Gerry left the old man's house knowing she couldn't come back for a second visit. His face — grey, his nose sharp — already had the mark of death on it.

However, with some gentle prompting from Fergus, she believed she had everything she needed, including Phillips's full name and a possible means of contacting him. He had corroborated Fergus's story, and had even managed to put his signature to it; there was little to add. She felt sorry for Fergus, who would be losing a good friend.

Having dropped Fergus off, she rang the office to inform Kate of the successful outcome of her visit. Trevor answered, saying that she and Tony had gone to interview a relative of Mel Dennis's.

Gerry worried about the advisability of the boss going out like this, even in broad daylight. True, they'd been over to the mortuary together this morning to speak to Fergus Winter, but that was only up the road, and it was a place they knew like the back of their hand. This was different. And in all likelihood the stalker was watching the station, waiting for just such an opportunity.

'Trevor,' she said, 'would you give me the address of this relative? I need to talk to the boss, so I can go and meet them there.'

'Hold on a sec. I know Tony wrote it down somewhere.' There was a pause while he went to find it. 'Here we are. It's the grandmother, someone called Enid Houghton. She lives in Knighton House on Fenfleet Lane, just outside Reedmere Village.'

Gerry thanked him and turned the car around. It wasn't far, and at least she'd have the boss within sight.

CHAPTER EIGHTEEN

The police car swung into the longest gravel drive that Kate had ever seen outside a stately home. 'Well, I'm not sure what I was expecting, but it was certainly not this,' she said when the old house came into view. 'It's massive.'

'They said it was big, but I didn't expect it to be quite so huge,' Tony said. 'Mel's family must be rolling in it.'

'I'm not so sure about that,' Kate said. 'Look at the state of the gardens; even the drive is full of weeds. I wouldn't mind betting that grand house has seen better days too.'

PC Peter Dawson, their escort driver, drew up outside the front entrance to the rambling old property, which on closer inspection badly needed a lot of money thrown at it.

'It's been split up into flats, hasn't it?' Kate said. 'Look. Practically every window has different curtains, and there's any number of cars parked around the side. I'm guessing our Enid can't bear to sell it so she's resorted to the expedient of renting rooms out.'

They were about to get out of the car when Kate's phone rang. 'Hi, Gerry. Where are you?'

'A few miles from Knighton House, boss. I wanted to let you know what Fergus's friend told me, so I'll join you there. See you in ten.'

Kate smiled to herself. Gerry hadn't fooled her; whatever the old guy had said could have waited till they got back. Gerry was concerned for Kate's safety. How lucky she was to have such loyal colleagues.

She made for the steps leading up to the massive front door. The sight of the ruined old house and the thought of Enid's struggles to hold onto it made Kate feel sad. But she also sensed a slight sinister undertone. Come on, she told herself, it's just an old property in need of more attention than the owner can afford.

But Tony was asking her a question. 'Do we try the main door? Only it looks unused.'

'Excuse me, officers!'

Kate turned to see an elderly gentleman marching towards them.

'Major Arthur Montgomery, a resident. May I be of assistance?'

'Detective Inspector Kate Carter, sir. We are looking for Enid Houghton,' she said, noting with amusement the emphasis on "Major".

'Ah, I see.' He hesitated. 'Er, may I have a quick word before I show you up to her apartment?'

Slightly puzzled, Kate followed the major around the front of the house to a smaller side door.

'Sorry about the trek,' said the major, 'but the front door jammed months ago, and we're still waiting for a carpenter to come and sort it out.'

He led the way in, and they followed him down a long, gloomy corridor with several doors leading off to the side, until they finally reached what was presumably the main entrance hall.

'If you would step into my apartment for a moment, I'll explain.' Major Montgomery held open a door.

Kate and Tony entered what would have once been the reception hall. Impressive, high-ceilinged, it was almost regal.

'Please, do take a seat. May I present my wife, Lottie? She and I were Knighton House's first paying guests.'

Kate suppressed a smile at the term "paying guests", and turned to greet a lady of elegant bearing, who had one of those smiles known as "charming".

'We'll remain standing if you don't mind, sir. We are anxious to speak with Miss Houghton, and we don't have a lot of time.'

Arthur Montgomery took a breath. 'Inspector, Enid Houghton is a splendid woman, but her life has been, shall we say, traumatic. She is no longer strong, and I am very afraid that a visit from the police may seriously affect her, er, mental balance.'

Kate groaned inwardly. Just what they needed.

'It may help you to know that her daughter and son-in-law were killed suddenly in a ghastly car accident, followed not long after by the death of her granddaughter, who was only in her teens. This series of tragedies destroyed her, Inspector. To this day, she is unable to speak about what happened, even to us who are her closest friends. To be honest, I have no idea how she keeps going, while, on top of it all, she has this great house to manage.'

Kate regarded them speculatively for a moment or two. By rights, she shouldn't tell them the purpose of their visit since it was a police matter and didn't concern them. But they looked so upset, she relented. 'We have some questions to ask her about her granddaughter, Amelia.' The major opened his mouth to protest, but Kate held up her hand. 'It's unavoidable, I'm afraid.'

Lottie sighed. 'Oh dear. Well, I'm not sure how much success you will have, Inspector. As my husband said, Miss Houghton has never yet been able to bring herself to even mention the girl's name.'

'Nevertheless, we have to try. The matter is urgent,' Kate said.

'In that case, might I suggest that one of us goes with you?' Arthur Montgomery said. 'It may help to have someone she knows present.'

'I don't see why not,' said Kate. 'In that case I should tell you that we are investigating a series of murders, the victims of which were all connected to Amelia.'

Lottie's hand flew to her mouth. 'Goodness gracious! Was Amelia murdered then? Is that why Enid never mentions her?'

Even we don't know the answer to that, Kate thought. She told the couple that they were looking for information about friends and other people connected to Amelia.

'Perhaps, then, if you and I went in alone, it might be a little less intimidating for her,' Arthur said.

Kate agreed. 'Why don't you stay here then, Tony. Perhaps Mrs Montgomery can give you some background details about Miss Houghton and the house. I'll be fine with the major, and our PC can wait in the hall to stop anyone else going up. Okay?'

Tony looked dubious; she guessed he was thinking about the order not to leave her alone for a second. Nevertheless, she could see the sense in what the major was suggesting.

As she followed Montgomery out into the hall, a man came hurrying down the corridor in their direction.

'Arthur! There's a police car outside. There's not a problem, is there? Are you and Lottie all right?'

'Don't worry, Barney,' said the major. 'The detective here has just come to have a few words with Enid.' He turned to Kate. 'This is Barney Capstick, who's soon to be our new neighbour.'

The man called Barney regarded her with an interest which quickly turned to consternation. He remained staring at her until she was forced to ask him if he was all right. 'Oh, er, yes. Sorry. It's just that you reminded me of someone.' He turned and almost ran back down the corridor.

'Strange young man,' she murmured, watching him go.

'Not like him at all, dash it. Barney's actually a jolly nice young fellow. Going to bring some new life to this garden, you know.'

'He's got his work cut out then,' said Kate. 'It's a jungle out there, I hope he owns a machete.'

'He'll do it,' said Arthur. 'He has vision, and he's a bit of an artist in his way.'

Kate wondered. He had looked at her as if he had seen a ghost. Anyway, she had bigger things to think about now. 'Okay, Major, how do you think we should approach Mrs Houghton so as not to cause her too much distress?'

'It's *Miss* Houghton actually. She brought up her daughter all on her own, and made a damned fine job of it too. But as to how we tackle this, perhaps I might broach the subject, then hand over to you. If you could see your way to being as tactful as possible? I'll try and smooth any troubled waters as we go.' As they spoke, they had been climbing a flight of wide, and rather worn, wooden stairs. 'The top floor is hers; no paying guests up here, oh no.'

Up here the house still retained a little of its former opulence. Heavy gold-framed paintings and ornate carved furniture lined the landing. They came to a halt outside a big double door. 'Used to be a reception room,' he whispered. Kate pictured a Miss Haversham sitting at a wedding feast table draped in cobwebs and couldn't help smiling.

Almost reverentially, Arthur tapped at the door. 'Enid? Enid, my dear, may we come in? I have someone here who would like to speak to you.'

After a few long seconds, the door opened to reveal an Enid Houghton who was nothing at all like the picture the major had painted of her.

Kate was caught off guard by a pair of piercing, suspicious eyes. Tearing her own eyes away, she saw that Miss Houghton was tall and thin to the point of gauntness. Her long grey hair was caught up in a bun, wisps of which fell about her hollow cheeks. She faced them, erect as the major. To Kate, she looked like a human replica of the house; an old and neglected beauty.

'Enid, this is Detective Inspector Carter,' said the major. 'There is no need to get anxious, she simply wishes to ask for your help.'

The baleful expression gave way to something like despair. This was no Miss Haversham, but even so, an air of deep sadness pervaded the room.

Enid gestured towards a couple of chairs. Meekly, Kate and Arthur sat down. After a few seconds, Arthur proceeded to explain that the name of her granddaughter had come up in relation to some very unfortunate recent events.

'I have no wish to cause you any distress, Miss Houghton,' Kate continued, 'but we believe that someone close to Amelia may be involved in a number of serious crimes that have been committed recently. All I need from you are names of her old friends, or other people she spent time with. I wouldn't be here if this weren't of the utmost importance.'

Enid Houghton said nothing, while a stream of different expressions swept across her gaunt features. Then she gave a tremulous sigh. 'There were three people she spent all her time with. Their names are seared into my memory, because if it weren't for them, she would still be alive today. They are Stephen Clarke, Toni Shields and Sean Raynor. Find them, and you need look no further.'

Kate's heart sank. 'Then you can't have heard. Miss Houghton, all three are dead.'

'I see. Well, if what you say is true, then I can only say I'm very pleased.'

'But, Enid, my dear,' Arthur said. 'You must have more than that to tell the inspector. If these people are all dead, you have to help the police catch whoever killed them.'

'We believe that someone by the name of Carl Pennington was a former boyfriend of Amelia's. What can you tell me about him?' Kate asked.

Miss Houghton almost smiled. 'Oh no, it wasn't Carl. He was indeed infatuated with Amelia, and took her death badly — he even contacted me a couple of times, few others did — but not long afterwards, his company offered him a six-month contract in Vietnam, and to my knowledge, he's there still.'

This left Kate with no more names to follow up. 'Can you think of anyone who cared deeply enough for Amelia to take revenge on the three people I mentioned? Those relatives of her father's, for example, who took her in after the death of her parents. Could they have something to do with it?'

'Ha! They only took her in to get her away from me. They never loved her, not the way I did.' Her voice trembled. 'They said living here was bad for her, a young woman shouldn't be cooped up miles from anywhere with no one but an elderly woman for company. What they really wanted was for me to die, and for Amelia to inherit Knighton House. They didn't know Amelia had overheard them plotting to get their hands on it. They intended to sell it to a hotel chain. Over my dead body.'

Kate sighed. This was going nowhere. Visions of Smithson taking over and making a mess of the case rose into her mind. She stood up and handed one of her cards to Miss Houghton. 'Please ring me if anyone else occurs to you.'

Enid Houghton received it in silence.

Outside in the corridor, Arthur stared at the closed door for a moment. 'Well. I've never heard Enid talk like that in all the time we've known her. If you don't mind, I'll just pop back in and make sure she's all right.'

'Of course,' Kate said. 'I'm sure it was very traumatic for her; it must have brought back some terrible memories.'

After Arthur had gone back inside, she stood silently, and a few moments later she heard the sound of soft sobbing.

CHAPTER NINETEEN

Gerry stopped at the end of the drive and stared at the building looming ahead. So this was Knighton House. She shivered. You'd never find her living in such a monstrosity.

She parked next to the police vehicle, got out and made for the front door. On closer inspection, she realised that trying to get in that way would be a futile endeavour. She ran back down the steps and around the side of the building where she almost collided with a man in jeans and a hoodie. 'Oops, sorry. Have you any idea how someone gets into this place?'

He gave her a crooked smile. 'The front door is buggered. Old lady Houghton said she can't afford the work it needs just yet, so we have to go round the side.'

We? 'You live here?'

'Yes, up there.' He pointed to an upstairs window. 'My name's Barney.'

Gerry stuck out a hand. 'Gerry. I'm a detective sergeant. Pleased to meet you, Barney.'

She noticed that he gave her a rather odd look. Then people often did when she told them she was a police officer.

'What's going on?' asked Barney. 'There are already three of your mates in here, and another one in that cop car. I'm starting to get a bit worried.'

'Oh, it's just routine enquiries, nothing to be concerned about.' Poor guy, he looked really anxious. Gerry smiled at him. 'Have you lived here long?'

'Not really.' He waved a hand at the gardens. 'I'm just about to start getting the gardens back to how they used to be.'

'Whew!' exclaimed Gerry. 'How long's that going to take?'

His answering laugh was pleasant and friendly. Gerry was already beginning to warm to him. 'I don't mind how long it takes, there's nothing I'd rather do. Miss Houghton desperately wants a bit of the past back, and besides, if I do a good job of it, I'll get a warmer flat. That's worth a lot.'

Gerry laughed. 'Well, good luck with that. Now I'd better go and look for my boss. Have you seen her anywhere?'

'I think she's up with Enid Houghton. I also saw her talking to Arthur Montgomery. I can take you to his flat if you like?' But he remained standing. 'Can I ask you something?'

'Sure.'

'That boss of yours. Who is she?'

'She's a detective inspector, her name's Kate Carter. Why?'

'Oh, nothing really. I just thought I recognised her, but I must have been mistaken. Anyway, the side entrance is just over there.' He pointed.

'She lives locally,' Gerry said, 'so you might have seen her around.' A strange expression flitted across Barney's face for a moment. 'Thanks, Barney. You take care, and good luck with your project.'

Gerry watched him walk away. She would have another talk to that young man before she left.

'Hi, Sarge.' Tony emerged from the door. 'The boss is still upstairs talking to the old lady who owns the place. Do you know what one of the residents told me? Amelia Dennis is buried right here in the grounds. What do you reckon to that?'

Gerry reckoned it was a bit creepy. The idea of a burial ground on the estate sounded rather Gothic to her.

'Not only that, but old Enid Houghton tends it with her own hands — cuts the grass and puts fresh flowers there every week. It's like a sort of shrine in the middle of this jungle.' Tony waved a hand at the gardens, which did indeed resemble a jungle.

'I suppose I can understand it,' Gerry said. 'At least she's nearby.' The thought of tending Nathan's grave almost made her heart stop. 'Anyway, I reckon I'll go and join the boss. Where is she exactly?'

'Right at the top of the house. There's this major bloke who's friendly with Enid Houghton, and he's gone up with her. Apparently, the old girl is a bit flaky, and he thought she might be more at ease with a woman. So, here I am, hanging around down here till they finish.'

'Well, last time I looked, I was a woman too, so maybe I'll risk it,' Gerry said.

Tony shrugged. 'Why not?'

She found the constable waiting at the foot of the stairs. 'Hello, Peter. They're still up there then?'

'I heard a door open a while back,' he said, 'but no one's come down.'

'Second floor, is it?' she asked.

'That's right. Want me to go up with you?' Peter asked.

'No, you're okay. I'll be back in a minute.'

Taking the stairs two at a time, Gerry reached a long, poorly-lit landing that stretched ahead of her towards a pair of double doors. Lined with paintings, Regency chairs and gilded mirrors, it had obviously once been magnificent. Now, however, it was merely shabby. She hesitated for a second outside the doors, then knocked and went in. An elderly man stood beside a chair with his hand resting on the shoulder of a seated woman, presumably Miss Houghton, but no Kate.

'Sorry to barge in like this. I'm DS Wilde, and I'm looking for DI Carter.'

The man looked across at her, frowning. 'But she left here fifteen minutes ago.' Then he smiled. 'I expect you missed each other.'

'But we couldn't have.' Gerry swallowed. 'The officer stationed at the bottom of the stairs told me no one has gone up or down.'

The man, whom she guessed to be the major bloke Tony had mentioned, gave Miss Houghton a final pat on the shoulder and came over to Gerry. 'She must have used the back stairs for some reason, though I can't think why.'

'Did she say where she was going?' Gerry asked.

'Just that she wanted to speak to the other detective. Enid was a little upset, so I stayed with her. Maybe your DI stopped off at my apartment.'

Gerry followed him down the stairs, pausing on the first-floor landing. There was a chance she'd met up with one of the residents and was talking to them. She called out Kate's name. No answer. Had they been followed to Knighton House? Had the stalker seen his chance and taken it?

Now seized by a real panic, she ran the rest of the way down, leaving a bemused Arthur Montgomery standing at the door to his apartment. 'Where's the DI?' she panted as soon as she caught sight of the others. They shrugged. Kate Carter was nowhere to be seen.

While they looked on, increasingly horrified, she pulled out her phone and rang Arun Desai. 'I need help, sir, and fast. She's been out of sight for fifteen, maybe twenty minutes. He must have been watching the station, and I think he's taken her.' She stopped for a second and caught her breath. 'And, sir? Please don't let Tom Carter know what's happening.'

* * *

In less than half an hour Knighton House was the centre of a massive police search. Cars were stationed at the main gate, others at the entry to the barns and outbuildings, still others lined the boundary to the estate. It soon became clear to Arun that he had a serious logistical problem on his hands. The place was a maze, a warren of corridors and passageways leading to countless rooms or ending nowhere at all.

He had commandeered the main hall, along with the Montgomerys' apartment, as a command centre. Major Arthur Montgomery's military background was proving invaluable. Calmly and succinctly, he handed out directions and told them all they needed to know about the house, its occupants and the various uses the outbuildings had been put to.

Every so often someone rushing past would glance over at the white-faced man seated, his hands gripping the armrests, in one of the Montgomerys' chairs, an untouched mug of tea at his side. Arun had chosen to ignore Gerry's request to not tell Kate's husband. If — God forbid — the worst happened to her, how would he ever look Tom Carter in the face and tell him he'd been kept in the dark?

Every minute that passed with no news, Arun grew more and more despondent. He, of all people, knew the statistics; knew that the longer she remained missing, the slimmer the chances of finding her alive.

* * *

Gerry, along with two uniformed officers, had just finished searching yet another outbuilding. This one was being used to pack handmade pottery for distribution. Just like the ones before it, there was no place here to hide anything, let alone a woman.

'DS Wilde, can I have a word, please?' It was Barney, hovering in the doorway, an anxious expression on his face. 'I hear your DI has gone missing. They said she was being threatened by someone. Is that right?'

'Yes, that's right. Why? Do you know something?'

He appeared to hesitate. 'I'm not sure . . . but there's something I think you should see.' He turned and headed for the main house, Gerry and the two uniforms at his heels.

'We need a key to Flat One,' said Barney, opening the side door. 'Miss Houghton should have the spare.'

Gerry sent one of the constables to get it from her. 'I don't care if she throws a fit, just get me that key. All right?' She turned to Barney. 'What's this about, Barney? Who lives in Flat One?'

'A man named Eric Payne. He's moving out soon, and I'll be moving in. It's bigger and much nicer than mine.' He blushed, embarrassed. 'The thing is, I'd never actually been into it, so . . . well, I was checking the trellis on the wall next to it, and I had a quick peek in through the windows.'

'Come on. What did you see?' asked Gerry.

'I really want you to see it,' Barney said, 'in case I've made a terrible mistake.'

'And you're sure he's not home? I'm going to have to knock first, so if you don't want to get involved you need to tell me what I'm looking for.'

'I'm sure.'

Just then, a panting Peter returned with a key.

Taking a deep breath, she rapped sharply on the door. 'Police! Mr Payne, we need to talk to you.'

No answer. She tried again.

Meeting yet more silence, she slowly unlocked the door and pushed it open. As far as she could see, the flat was empty. She could also see why Barney was keen to move in. It was tastefully decorated, had semi-decent furniture, and a beautiful fireplace set in a wood-panelled wall. But more than all this was the fact that there was no indication that anyone lived here. No knick-knacks, no personal items, no clothes. The room was bare of anything except the furniture.

'Looks like he's already moved out,' remarked Gerry.

'But I saw him go out this morning,' Barney said, 'and there was a half-packed suitcase on the sofa when I peeked in. Maybe he's been back and moved all his stuff in the bedroom ready to finish packing.' He nodded to the door.

Gerry pushed open the door and stopped abruptly on the threshold. 'What the f—?'

A double bed, and an old-fashioned wardrobe. Two packed cases sat on the bed, along with a holdall. At the foot of the bed was a chest of drawers, with an anglepoise lamp that had been left on, its beam aimed at a large poster-size framed photograph. A close-up of Kate Carter.

Along with the lamp, Gerry saw a collection of objects on the chest of drawers. On closer inspection, these turned out to be a crumpled sheet of paper, a battered box of chocolates and a child's coloured picture of her mummy. She stared at them for a few moments, and then, suddenly galvanised, ran in search of Arun Desai.

CHAPTER TWENTY

Bound hand and foot, Kate struggled to sit up. She was in a dank, windowless bare room. She had a dim recollection of leaving Enid Houghton's apartment and hearing Arthur's footsteps behind her. Only it wasn't Arthur. As she turned to speak to him, she felt a sharp pain in the side of her neck like a bee sting. Then a hand, clamped over her mouth, and someone holding onto her tightly as she swayed and lost her balance. After that, things got weird. She had the strangest recollection of being pushed right through a solid wall! And now she was here.

Gradually, her mind began to clear. She knew just what had happened. The stalker. The stalker had her.

Kate shut her eyes tight and forced herself to think straight. How, when he supposedly knew nothing about the investigation she was leading, did he know she was coming here? She was absolutely certain they hadn't been tailed. How did he even get up the stairs to grab her when there was a PC at the bottom keeping watch? Had he tapped her phone? Was it someone inside the station, someone who had overheard her mention Knighton House? Surely not. But then, what did you really know about people?

She had no idea where in the house she was, and nothing in the room gave her a clue. Her phone, of course, was gone from her pocket. However, she was pretty certain that she was still in Knighton House. She had a memory of being half carried, half dragged down some stairs, but not of being put into a vehicle.

A sudden wave of nausea made her wonder what he'd given her to knock her out. It couldn't be anything too toxic, since her head was already beginning to clear. She took a few deep breaths, grateful for the fact that she hadn't been gagged. Then it dawned on her that not having her mouth covered meant she wouldn't be heard if she called for help. So, where was she? And where the hell was the man who had put her here?

She spent some minutes trying to evaluate her chances of escape but soon realised it was hopeless. For some reason, she wasn't afraid, and that puzzled her. It was almost a relief, or at least a kind of inevitability. The waiting was over. No more looking over her shoulder. No more fear of going anywhere alone. Soon, she'd know who this bastard was, and why he was hellbent on taking her away from the family she loved.

The thought of her family dispelled all the resignation she'd been feeling and gave her the will to survive. She would beat this bastard using every trick in the book, every manoeuvre learned in her many years of experience. She wasn't a policewoman for nothing. In her time, she'd managed to outwit the wicked, the cruel, the insane. This man, whoever he was, would be no worse. She just had to find a way into his mind, and manipulate him into letting her go. That, or she'd never see her family again.

* * *

Meanwhile, Gerry was beside herself. She had experienced her fair share of bad situations, but none had involved a person she was close to. And Kate was a dear friend.

She ran through all she had been taught about this kind of situation. But nothing had prepared her for how to act when someone had been apparently spirited away into thin air. She just couldn't fathom out how he could possibly have done it.

For some reason the thought of Cold Colin sprang into her mind. She called him and told him Kate had been taken, and that she feared for her safety. Wasting no time in asking questions, he set off at once for Knighton House. On seeing the picture of Kate on Eric Payne's wall, his first act was to remove the cases and bag from Flat One and close it off in preparation for a comprehensive forensic examination. He carried the luggage over to the centre of operations, laid it out on a large sheet of plastic and removed the contents, item by item.

Enid Houghton's rooms having been thoroughly inspected, Gerry joined the search. She was just about to trudge yet again up the steep stairs, this time to check the attic, when Barney appeared, carrying a large box file. 'It's Arthur Montgomery's research on the house,' he explained. 'He did a lot of it at one time, and he lent it to me after I told him I was interested. I was sifting through it the other night, and I came across an old plan of Knighton House. It shows stairways that are never used now, and passageways joining different parts of the building that no one even knows about. The house was originally built in the late 1600s, and there was a farmstead here even before that. I think it has hidden places, DS Wilde. You need to talk to Arthur and Miss Houghton.'

Gerry took it from him and headed back downstairs to Arthur's apartment.

'What he says is true, Knighton House did have a lot of passageways, like all old buildings of this age, but most have been sealed up.' Arthur stared at the old map. 'I've never used it myself, but Enid once told me about a staircase at the back of the house, formerly used by the servants. It led down to what used to be the main kitchen. She said the door to the stairs has been locked for donkey's years, but we could check. Shall I show you where it is?'

Gerry was already heading for the door, with Peter close behind, when a voice stopped her in her tracks.

'DS Wilde. Please, wait a moment.'

She turned and saw Colin looking at her. His face was very pale.

'I found this. It was in one of Eric Payne's cases.' His hand shaking slightly, he held up an old forty-five rpm record. 'It's from 1964.'

She stared at it, uncomprehending.

'There is a small notebook with it with a list of names, all crossed out, apart from one: Alexander Phillips, with an address in France. Considering that there is a passport in the holdall, I'd suggest the occupant of Flat One is your killer.'

'And the name that hadn't been crossed out—' whispered Gerry.

'The man who founded the Sixty-four Club,' said Colin. 'And one last thing. I expect someone has been checking the PNC for the name Eric Payne? And they found nothing.'

'Not a mention, nor with the DVLA or on the electoral register,' Gerry said, with a sick feeling that she knew where this was going.

'The name on the passport is Jude Comfrey,' said Colin.

Gerry stared at him. 'Sorry, Colin, I can't quite take this in. Are you telling me that Kate's stalker is our murderer?'

'I'm afraid I am.'

Gerry whirled round and ran back to where Arun was directing the search. She began to tell him what Colin had found when Tom, whose presence she had completely forgotten, broke in.

Getting to his feet, he advanced towards them. 'Enough! I'm coming with you. There's no way I can sit here drinking bloody tea while my wife is being held captive by a murderer.'

Gerry glanced helplessly at Arun, who nodded. 'He's right, let him go with you. I'll deal with the consequences.'

As Tom started towards the door, Arun held him back. 'Tom. I've put my job on the line for you. Do *not* do anything that would expose you, or one of my officers, to danger. This is a police matter. My people are trained to deal with situations like this without losing control. They know what to do. Let them. Okay?'

Tom nodded, but Gerry wondered if he'd even heard. How could he not wade in and try to save a wife in mortal danger?

* * *

Arthur led them up the stairs to the second floor, but instead of going towards Miss Houghton's rooms, he turned left at the top of the stairs. There, they passed what he told them was the established back staircase, and continued on, through a door, into a narrower corridor. 'This was the east wing. Up until the Victorian era, it accommodated a nursery and a schoolroom. It's no longer in use, so go carefully.'

Wishing the old guy would leave out the history, Tom nevertheless listened to every word. His knowledge of the house could well lead them to the place where Kate was being held.

Arthur was right to warn them to tread warily. The entire wing was in a terrible state. The plaster from the walls had crumbled, leaving piles of detritus scattered across the floor.

Ahead of him, Gerry suddenly exclaimed, 'Look. This stuff has been disturbed. I think they came this way.'

'It makes sense,' Arthur said. 'But only if it's still accessible. If it is, he could have taken her down the old servants' stairs I showed you, thereby avoiding the police and anyone else who was about. Although I can't think how he knew about them. This is the first time I've been up here; this part of the house is strictly out of bounds to residents.'

Tom hurried after them, fighting his way through cobwebs thick enough to trap you as if you were a fly, while the intricate carving in the panelling was obscured by creeping mould.

'Yes, they definitely came this way,' called back Gerry. 'I can see scuff marks in the dust, and there's a candle sconce here that's been knocked off kilter not long ago.'

Tom pictured a faceless killer dragging his precious Kate along this ghastly corridor and his eyes filled with tears. He fought them back. He could let go later, now was not the time.

'It's down here.' Arthur took a sharp right turn, then stopped at a door. 'Someone's unlocked it!' He opened it and revealed a flight of stairs. 'They lead to a small lobby outside the old kitchens,' he said. 'They have now been partitioned into storerooms, a boiler room and a utility area where Enid was planning to install washing machines and a clothes dryer, but the work was never completed because the money ran out. The old butler's pantry and the game larder still exist as they once were.' He frowned. 'And the wine cellar is still there. That really is kept locked. Enid told me the key never leaves her possession. Steep stone steps and no electricity could mean a serious accident.'

In single file they took the ancient stone steps, worn smooth by the feet of countless servants going about the business of the house. There was a small landing halfway down that Tom assumed led to the first floor, but it was clear from the smudges in the dust on the handrail that they needed to continue to the ground floor.

'Is there a door from the stairs to the outside, Arthur?' Peter called over his shoulder.

'Not from the lobby. As far as I can remember, you'd have needed to go through the kitchen area to the tradesman's entrance. There was a door close to the old stairs, but Enid sealed it up, this part of the house being so unsafe.'

'So, they couldn't have used this route to escape the house?' Peter said.

Arthur thought for a moment. 'No. Unless I'm very wrong, he had somewhere in mind to hide your DI Carter and used these stairs to avoid detection.'

By now they were all in the lobby. Tom stood a little apart, fists clenched, trying not to cry. This was taking too long. She could be dead by now.

Someone laid a hand on his arm.

'Hang on in there,' said Gerry softly. 'We'll find her.' Giving his arm a squeeze, she turned to Arthur. 'Okay, Major. We're relying on you. Where would he go?'

For a moment the old man's face assumed a pleading expression. He wanted to return to his fireside, and not have to assume this burden. Then he straightened his shoulders. 'Right. Let's find a flat surface for this.' He pulled the old map out of his pocket and unfolded it. 'There are only two or three places in this part of the house where you could conceal someone. It has to be one of them, since the rest have been searched. Now, let's see where they are . . .'

CHAPTER TWENTY-ONE

Still, he hadn't appeared. Kate struggled endlessly with her bonds, but he had used heavy-duty nylon cable ties, and her effort simply tightened them further. She couldn't believe he had left her here to die; surely he wanted more than that from her. Meanwhile, there was nothing to do but wait.

It hadn't taken her long to go over every inch of the room. The walls were stone, the heavy door fitted tight. There was no point knocking or screaming. In the dim light of the single candle lamp, her resolve began to wane, and fear started to creep in. Maybe she'd die here from lack of oxygen; the room was small enough.

Trying not to give way to despair, she squeezed her eyes shut and recited the names of her children, her pets. Tom. Oh, Tom! Suddenly, she froze.

'Kaa-tie. Kaa-tie.'

She hadn't even heard him come in.

He stood before her, and Kate knew him at once. Gerry had been right. Jude Comfrey. The man with the curious eyes.

In the confines of the small room, he seemed taller, more of a presence than she remembered. The eyes were the same though. Pale as those of a blind man, they were nonetheless piercing. She shrank beneath their gaze.

To her surprise, he squatted on the floor in front of her — not too close — and shook his head. 'At last! Back together again after so long. You're as beautiful as ever.' He sighed. 'I had such plans for us, Kate. All ruined now, thanks to you and your friends. So, what to do?'

'You could let me go,' she said in a voice she didn't recognise as her own. 'It would be better for you in the long run. Apologise, and no harm done. I don't know why you feel the way you do about me, but as long as no one gets hurt, we can just go our separate ways. I won't even press charges.'

'Oh, you think it's that simple, do you?' He gave a hollow laugh. 'I can't let that happen, not after all this time.'

'Look, Jude. Suppose we walk out of here together. I swear I'll play it down. I'll say I overreacted. I'm sorry if you think I've egged you on, or, I don't know, made you think I'm not happy at home. But, you see, that's not the case.'

Kate watched for his reactions. She could be making things worse, or . . . maybe there was a chance that he wasn't too far gone to reach.

'You are so very lovely,' he said, his voice choked with emotion, 'but you have no idea what's at stake here. I've been through hell to get you where you are now — with me at last.'

'Please, Jude. Imprisoning a police officer carries a heavy penalty. It's abduction, for heaven's sake! You could get up to twelve years for holding me here like this. Just let me go and I'll speak up for you. You haven't hurt me, that's the main thing. Anything you do now can either make it easier, or, well, I may not be able to help you.'

'Stop it, Kate, please. You know nothing about this situation. What, you imagine us walking out of here arm-in-arm? Never!'

It seemed there was more to this man than she knew about. Having exhausted all her pleas for reason, she could do nothing now but wait for him to make the next move.

He rose to his feet and began pacing the small room like a caged animal.

'Damn you and your cronies! It wasn't meant to be like this. They've broken into my room, they've taken my things! There's policemen swarming all over the place. And I can't keep you here much longer; this room is not suitable for what I have in mind for us.'

Faced with this sudden display of rage, she was at a loss as to how to respond. She remained silent, wondering how he knew that his things had been taken. It could only mean that somehow her friends had found out that Jude Comfrey was a resident in Knighton House. That being the case, they'd be tearing the place apart in their search for her — and him.

'If, as you say, the place is full of police officers, there's no way you'll get out, either alone or with me. Please, Jude, do as I say. Even if I don't understand your situation, I can help you. I can.'

He sank down and sat with his back against the door. 'Even you, lovely Kate, can't help me out of three charges of murder.'

Murder? What was he saying? Who had he killed? Not her children! 'Who . . . ?'

'It's all right, Kate. It's not your children. I told you before I didn't care about them, it's you alone I love.' He regarded her thoughtfully. 'And I can get us out of here. I know every inch of Knighton bloody House, I've spent the past year mapping every nook and cranny. I must know it better than the man who built it. But we can escape more easily at night, so we'll just have to wait a while.'

While he spoke, Kate saw the corner of her royal-blue phone cover sticking out of his jacket pocket. Dammit. If only she could get hold of it. But how, with her wrists so tightly bound? Then it came to her. There *was* a way she could help herself.

Abruptly, Jude stood up. 'I must leave you for a while. There is something I have to do. But don't worry, I'll be back.' He leaned forward and gently stroked her cheek with his finger. 'I can hardly bear to leave you, now you are here.'

Not wanting to antagonise him, Kate managed not to flinch under his touch. 'But how can you do anything when the place is alive with police officers?'

Jude laughed. 'As I said, I know this place. They don't. I will move past them like a wraith, and they'll never even know I was there. You will too, when the time comes.'

Then he was gone. Kate let out a long breath. If there were secret corridors and passages, that would explain her strange impression of passing through a solid wall. It also explained why he was so confident of remaining unseen.

She wondered how long she had. There was one chance of getting help, and if she managed to pull it off, she might make it out alive.

* * *

By now, Gerry was on the verge of panic. With the aid of the map, they had checked three possible places where someone could be concealed, but all were empty and had obviously remained so for years. The last possibility was the cellar, but it was locked, and showed no signs of having been tampered with.

'Nevertheless,' Gerry said, 'it will have to be searched. Peter, leg it back to the old lady's rooms and ask her for the key to the wine cellar. If Comfrey knows this place as well as he seems to, there's a chance he stole that key and had a copy done. It doesn't look like it's been opened recently, but we can't just assume that's the case. And, Peter, if she refuses to give it to you, tell her we'll break the bloody thing down.'

By this stage, Tom looked as if he was about to explode with frustration. He was also very pale. 'Sorry, but I need some air,' he said. 'How the hell do I get out of this blasted place?'

'I'll take you,' said Arthur. 'It's not as far as you might think. There's an outside door that takes you into a courtyard where the tradespeople used to unload their goods.'

'Why don't we all go?' Gerry said. 'There's not much we can do here until Peter gets back.'

The fresh air felt good, but they were all too conscious of the precious time they were wasting. With every minute that passed, the chance that Kate had remained unharmed diminished.

'DS Wilde!'

Barney again. 'I've been looking everywhere for you. Look. I found this.'

He held out his hand. On his palm lay a keyring, or part of one. It was just the fob, and in it was a photograph of a dog.

'Let me see that!' Tom snatched it from Barney. 'That's Rodders, our Labrador! It was attached to the zipper on Kate's handbag. Where did you find it? Take us there, now!'

Barney told them he had found it in a covered walkway on the west side of the house. Immediately, Gerry told Peter's crewmate to call him on his radio. They would check the cellar after they'd seen the place where Barney had found the key fob.

They ran after Barney. 'Look,' he said. 'The plants along the border have been trodden on recently.'

'And there's a footprint there,' said Gerry, pointing. 'You can see from the imprint of the sole and heel which way they were heading. And it's in the opposite direction to the area we've been checking.' She pictured a man dragging his victim along the narrow path, and stepping occasionally into the border. 'Where does this lead?'

Barney spread his hands.

'Along the back to the west side of the house,' said Arthur. 'The staff would have come this way when they brought refreshments out to the owners, if they were entertaining outside. It ends at the edge of the house, but there's another pathway that continues out to the stables and the gardens.'

'Then he may not have kept her in the house at all,' said Tom.

'Maybe not. What if . . .' Gerry was thinking aloud. 'What if he had to get her off that second-floor landing, and when he saw us down in the hall, he took her down the back stairs, and then out and around the house.'

'But what about all the marks we saw in that old corridor in the east wing?' asked Tom.

'That could well be a false trail,' said Gerry. 'Clever. You met Eric Payne, Arthur. Did he know you were interested in the history of Knighton House?'

'Yes,' he said. 'We even discussed it on a few occasions. It was the only time he seemed mildly interested in anything.'

Clever indeed. Eric Payne — or rather, Jude Comfrey — had realised that they would eventually discover that Amelia was the key to the murders. And who would they want to interview? Her grandmother, of course. 'He planned this! He knew Kate would come here. He left a false trail for us to follow because he knew Arthur was at least aware of the deserted east wing.'

'When all the time he'd taken her in the other direction,' added Tom. 'Oh my God! Maybe they've got away! She could be anywhere by now.'

'I don't think so. This is a massive old place with acres of grounds; there are any number of places he can hide her. Peter's crewmate swears no cars have gone down the drive. I'm sure she's still here; the problem is, how long for? He can't keep her hidden for ever.' Gerry shivered. 'If it was me, I'd wait till nightfall. It'll be easier then, he just has to wait for the right moment.'

Tom looked at his watch. 'That means we have less than two hours. We'll never do it, will we?'

Gerry met his gaze. 'We'll find her, even if it means dismantling this old house brick by brick.'

* * *

Back in Arthur's apartment, they found a distraught Arun.

'It's Miss Houghton, Gerry,' he said. 'She's collapsed. It must all have been too much for her. An ambulance is on its way, but I'm afraid it's too late. Lottie Montgomery is with her, along with Tony and a first responder, but it's not looking good.'

Gerry was sorry for the old lady, but right now, Kate was her priority. She told Arun of the footsteps Barney had seen in the flowerbed. 'Can we get as many officers as possible round to that side of the grounds? There are any number of places in that area where she could be hidden. Oh, and we still haven't checked the cellar. Peter went to fetch the key, but we haven't seen him since.'

'It was Peter who found her,' Arun said. 'The old lady was slumped in her chair, barely responsive. But you're right, we need to find that key. You go upstairs and see if you can find where she keeps her keys, and I'll direct the search parties to that part of the garden.'

'I know where her keys are kept,' said Arthur. 'I'll go with you. I should also check on my wife.'

'But, Gerry, surely that's a total waste of time.' Tom looked distraught. 'We should be out where we saw those tracks heading!'

Tom was close to breaking point, and she could hardly blame him. Time was running out. 'Just stay put, okay? I'll be back. And don't forget, Arun's got plenty of people. This is a big garden, but it isn't that big.' She looked at his anguished expression. 'Second thoughts, come with me. I don't want you tearing off and ripping the grounds to shreds.'

As they ascended the staircase, they were overtaken by two paramedics. Gerry pointed the way to Miss Houghton's rooms, and she, Arthur and Tom followed them inside.

The three of them stood back and watched the paramedics at work. But it was obviously too late for Enid Houghton.

Arthur went to his wife and put his arm around her shoulders.

'Poor Enid,' said Lottie. 'I couldn't have been gone more than a few minutes, and she wasn't alone.'

'So, who was with her?' asked Gerry.

'She said one of the other residents was coming in to bring something for her. She said he was on his way up, so I went to make tea and get her something to eat. She'd had nothing all day, and she said she felt faint.'

'Who was it, my dear?' asked Arthur.

'I don't know,' Lottie said. 'I never saw him. I was in the kitchen when I heard the door open, and I heard her tell him to come in. Whoever it was had gone when that nice police officer arrived, and he raised the alarm.'

Gerry saw one of the paramedics beckoning to her. 'We've done all we can here, now we need to get her to hospital, fast.' The medic lowered her voice. 'I'm afraid this isn't straightforward. We suspect she, er, ingested something.'

Gerry stared at her. 'What? Poison?'

'Looks that way.'

What next? By this time, Gerry felt like her head was about to explode. She told one of the constables to inform the superintendent of the paramedic's suspicions.

Had the old lady deliberately poisoned herself? It seemed unlikely. Who, then, had given it to her? Which one of the tenants had visited her just before she was taken ill? And if it was a deliberate act, why on earth kill a harmless old lady?

Kate should be here, heading up this damned investigation. Instead, she was one of the victims.

CHAPTER TWENTY-TWO

After hours of sitting on the cold floor of her cell, Kate had developed excruciating cramps in her legs. She tried to move her feet to relieve them, but the cable ties bit into her skin. Comfrey had been gone for so long she began to suspect that he'd been apprehended. Much as the thought of this pleased her, if he refused to say where he had hidden her, she'd have more than a pain in her legs to worry about.

Finally, she heard the key turn in the lock. He was back, carrying a blanket and a pillow. 'I'm sorry, it's going to be another hour before we can move out, so I brought these to make you a bit more comfortable.'

Comfrey draped the blanket around her shoulders and settled the pillow behind her head. It smelled surprisingly of lavender. He sat down on the floor, facing her. 'If I thought I could trust you, I'd untie your ankles. They must be hurting by now.'

'You needn't worry about me making a run for it,' she said. 'I'm so stiff, I can't even move.'

He said nothing to this, only gazed at her, until she was forced to break the silence. 'Why me?'

'We don't choose who we fall in love with, Kate. It just happens. And believe me, no one could ever love you like I do. Not your husband. The love I have for you is deeper than anything he could possibly feel. From the first moment I saw you in that interview room, I knew you were the one. When we've been together a while, you'll soon come to realise the truth of what I say. Then you'll never want another man.'

'Did you really kill people to make this happen?' she asked tentatively.

'It was death that brought us together in the first place, wasn't it?' he said.

'You mean the hit-and-run you witnessed?'

He laughed. 'Witness. That was one investigation you failed to get right, my dear. You see, I wasn't the witness. I was the driver.'

She exhaled. 'I see. There was one police officer who didn't believe your story. It looks like we should have paid more attention to him.'

He shrugged. 'Maybe you should have.'

'I must say, you were very convincing,' said Kate. 'But if it was an accident, why all the subterfuge? Unless you were speeding or driving dangerously, I doubt there would have been any charges laid.'

Jude Comfrey gave her a very odd look. 'Ah, but it wasn't an accident.'

'You mean it was intentional?'

'Totally. And it was a very successful hit, even though I say it myself. As I said, you know nothing about me or my circumstances.' He fell silent for a few seconds, as if he were waiting for her to comprehend. 'It's my job, Kate. It's what I do. So you see now why I can't just walk out of here and give myself up, don't you?'

Kate did. She also understood that she was in mortal danger.

'Don't be afraid,' he said soothingly. 'It's just a job. When you get to know me, you'll see what a good person I am.'

This was insane. 'You mentioned three murders. Was that hit-and-run one of them?'

'Oh no, I hadn't counted him. The three I spoke of were a completely different assignment. Actually, the contract was for four, but now I've finally found you, I'm going to call it a day.' He laughed. 'Number four has had a lucky escape.'

He leaned forward and stroked her arm. 'Think of it like this. You saved someone's life. Doesn't that make you feel good?'

Far from it. 'How can you be a contract killer and at the same time be the nice person you say you are? It doesn't add up.'

'Well, how do you do it?' he said. 'Simple. I compartmentalise. Just like you, I don't take my work home with me.' He checked his watch and stood up. 'Anyway, back to us. It's not too long before we have to leave, and I need to get you back on your feet. I will untie your ankles, but I don't think I can trust you not to run. Or to keep quiet. So unfortunately, that means I'll have to use the rest of what I gave you earlier.'

He produced a syringe, and before she had time to react, plunged the needle into her neck. In moments, Kate was back in that strange dream-world in which she was able to walk through walls.

* * *

As twilight descended over the surrounding countryside, Knighton House was illuminated like a beacon, lit up with halogen lights brought in so that the search could continue into the night.

Hopes for finding Kate were dwindling, the sombre mood of the gathered officers darkened further by the news that Enid Houghton had died. The hospital believed that she had taken Pentobarbital, a short-acting barbiturate normally used in euthanasia or assisted suicide.

Questions remained as to the identity of the caller Lottie had heard while she was in the kitchen.

Gerry's search party was back in the Montgomerys' apartment, helping themselves to a quick cup of coffee before returning to the hunt. Gerry was fast giving up hope. Maybe Tom had been right, and Comfrey had got Kate away before the estate was overrun with police.

Gerry was adding yet another spoonful of sugar into her coffee when she received a message on her phone. Assuming it was her mother yet again, she was tempted to ignore it. But, like most people, being a slave to her device meant she couldn't help taking a quick look. The teaspoon clattered to the floor. 'It's Kate! Everyone! I've got a message from Kate!' She read it properly, and her eyes widened. 'My God! She's sent her location!' Gerry raced over to the startled superintendent and thrust her phone at him. 'Sir! Look! We can track her.'

Arun was sceptical. 'Surely whoever has her will have taken her phone away. Maybe he's laying another false trail.'

'I don't think so.' It was Tom, peering over the super's shoulder to read the message. 'Just as we were leaving this morning, Kate said she'd forgotten her smartwatch, and went back for it. I clearly remember her shoving it into her trouser pocket just before she got in the car. He probably did take her phone, but she can send messages from her watch, especially if her phone is nearby.'

Gerry remembered Kate's embarrassment at being caught wearing such a costly watch. Right now, however, it could be saving her life. 'I don't quite get this. Sir, can you make it out?'

Arun stared at the message. 'Well, according to this, it looks as if she's only a few rooms away from where we are, but we've checked every single one.'

Lottie, who had been washing mugs at the sink, came toward them. 'I overheard what you said. Can I ask which room it is?'

'Somewhere near Flat One, Comfrey's flat,' said Arun.

Arthur appeared beside her. 'Then he really did do his homework on the place. Enid, bless her heart, told Lottie about a number of secret passageways, one of which was hidden behind the panelling in Flat One. Because that flat was always occupied, we never had an opportunity to investigate. It seems that Eric — I mean Jude Comfrey — did. And found it.'

'You mean they are somewhere behind these walls?' Arun stared incredulously at Arthur and Lottie.

'I certainly do,' said Arthur. 'According to Enid, there was a catch concealed in a carving on the panel nearest the fireplace.'

'She also said there might be other passages scattered around the house, though she wasn't sure. They could just have been stories,' Lottie said. 'But the one in Comfrey's flat definitely did exist, she'd even been inside it once, in her childhood, and—'

Before Lottie had finished speaking, Gerry and her team were heading for the door.

'Wait! You need this.' Arun held out her phone. 'The marker is moving east. And be on your guard. We know what he's capable of, so no heroics. Kate's life is at stake — and maybe yours too if you're not careful.'

'And take torches!' called Arthur.

Gerry paused in her headlong dash. They needed to be fast, but they also needed to think. 'Sir, can you get us an officer with a taser? And if I am able to radio you with Kate's location, maybe we should have a firearms unit available in case they break cover.'

'There's one about two minutes away. I requested it when we found out that the guy in Flat One was Comfrey.' He sent an officer off to find a constable with a taser. 'All right, Gerry, you can go, but wait for the taser. I'll have the firearms unit ready and awaiting your directions. And good luck.'

After some fumbling around the carving to find the catch, a section of panelling slid back to reveal a dark passageway that appeared to lead into another, wider one.

'Arthur's old map said nothing about this,' Gerry muttered, wishing the bloody taser would hurry up.

'You don't put secrets on a map, do you?' said Tony. 'These passages might have been built to hide contraband or something. We're not far from the North Sea here. I bet the house was used to conceal all manner of illegal goods smuggled across from mainland Europe.'

That made sense to Gerry. It also meant that one of the passages would lead out of the building.

The marker on her phone was slowly moving east, away from the main part of the house. 'Tony,' Gerry hissed, 'we'll have to get there soon, or we'll lose them.'

'Please, Gerry, let's go now!' Tom pleaded. 'If they get away, I could lose her forever.'

In her excitement over the message, Gerry had forgotten that Tom was still with them. He shouldn't be, but how could she ask him to stay behind? She called over her shoulder, 'Luke, wait until the taser arrives and follow us in. We'll keep radio silence unless it's absolutely necessary. We can't afford to let Comfrey hear us. We don't want him to know we have discovered his secret passages.'

She ducked, through the secret door and toward an unknown destination.

CHAPTER TWENTY-THREE

Kate was floating, as if she were treading water, held up by an arm around her waist, propelling her forward. Like a plane travelling through clouds, the atmosphere grew dense, then clear, then she passed from darkness to light, and back into darkness. A voice in her ear kept urging her forward, to make haste. What for? She was quite enjoying this dream, if that's what it was.

* * *

Gerry too was beginning to feel as if she was in a dream, although in her case, it was almost a nightmare. Enclosed spaces made her panic. At least there were lights. Comfrey had thought to hang battery lanterns to light his passage, but hadn't thought to turn them off, which helped their progress considerably. Another thing in their favour was that there were no other passages leading off the one they were following, so they had to be on the right trail. She believed that Tony had been right about contraband having been smuggled into the house, this passage being the route in and out. They just had to catch up with Comfrey before he made it to the exit.

She had lost the signal on her phone, but her last reading of the location marker told her they weren't far behind Kate. Luke, and two other officers with tasers, had now caught up with them, so all they could do was press on, and hope for an opportunity to separate Comfrey from Kate and take him down.

* * *

Back in the Montgomerys' apartment, Arun had tracked the progress of Kate's watch from his tablet as far as the point where the signal was lost. He sketched a diagram of the route and compared it with Arthur's old map, giving him the direction in which Comfrey was heading. They had no idea where the passage ended, except that it was east, towards the marshes and the Wash. Arthur got in touch with a local historian who confirmed that in the golden age of import smuggling on the East Coast, Knighton House had been the repository of massive amounts of "genever", over-proofed Dutch gin.

'Excuse me, sir. Could I take a look at those maps?'

The speaker was Barney Capstick. 'Sure. I understand you are hoping to restore the garden. That's quite a task.'

'I was,' said Barney glumly. 'But who knows what will happen now poor old Miss Houghton has passed.' He squinted at the maps and scratched his head. 'Mmm, I thought so. I wonder . . .'

'Come on, lad,' urged Arun. 'You've thought of something, haven't you?'

Arthur hurried over. 'What are you thinking, Barney?'

'Well, from the direction they are heading — east — out into the road, that leads to the coast, here.' He pointed to a spot just outside the boundary of the estate. 'A straight line takes us to the old folly, which is close to the perimeter of the grounds.'

'By Jove, lad. You're right!' exclaimed the major.

'And that means what?' asked Arun.

'I'd been wondering why it had been built just there,' said Barney. 'It serves no purpose, other than to give a vista, a view down the lawns to the house. But it's larger than your average folly, and has survived intact since the 1700s. I can't help but think that it did have a purpose, but we don't know what it was.'

'Barney's right,' said Arthur. 'The coast road is not far behind it, just about a hundred feet away through the trees that border the property. If there is a gateway, or an old entrance thereabouts, the smugglers could have brought their contraband into the folly.'

'You are saying that there might be a trapdoor or something that gives access to the secret passage?' said Arun.

'It's in the perfect position,' said Barney. 'It even has a view of the house, so the smugglers could make sure that the coast was clear. Someone in the house could have sent a signal telling them when it was safe to move the goods into the tunnel.' He stood back with an air of satisfaction.

'We must get a team there right away, and if there is indeed a trapdoor, we'll get the armed unit to it. We need to act fast if we're to arrive before Comfrey. I'll message Gerry as to where we believe they are heading.' He patted Barney on the shoulder. 'If this does prove to be the exit, you'll be the hero of the hour, Barney Capstick!'

* * *

Barney's supposition had been right. Shortly after the team sent to the folly discovered the entrance to the passage, hidden beneath one of the slabs covering the floor, Gerry's phone picked up a signal again. Kate was only a short distance from the folly. Leaving the other officers in place to block the way, should Comfrey panic and try to backtrack, Gerry retreated from the passage with Tom, and they hurriedly made their way to the folly.

The old, supposedly useless building was silent, enshrouded in darkness. Whoever emerged from the tunnel would have no idea that the folly was surrounded by police officers.

Arun, along with the officer in charge of the armed response unit, could only watch and wait. They had no idea of the state Kate would be in, or to what extent her movements were restrained, and her safety was paramount. In readiness, officers had been positioned around the folly, along the path to the boundary, and on both sides of an old gate that led out to the road.

Gerry had never been so tense, or so anxious. Everything depended on chance, and on what Comfrey would do next. The folly was too small inside to accommodate any officers without the risk of Comfrey spotting them, so they had no choice but to wait, and watch.

It seemed like forever, but in fact it wasn't long at all before she saw a shadowy figure appear in the doorway of the folly. Peering into the gloom, she realised that it was two people. Comfrey, supporting his captive and almost carrying her outside.

Gerry almost gasped. Kate was staggering, as if only partially conscious. What had he done to her? Gerry swallowed hard and continued to watch as Comfrey guided Kate out and onto the path that led to the gate.

Gerry could not see a weapon. There was certainly none in his hand. He had to use both to steer his unsteady captive away from the folly.

Their chance didn't come until captor and captive made it to the gate. Then, due to its age and years of disuse, Comfrey was obliged to leave Kate propped up against a tree while he lifted and dragged the gate open. As he turned back to her, he was suddenly illuminated in a blaze of light. Blinded, he staggered back and was immediately wrestled to the ground.

Gerry ran at once to Kate. One look told her that her friend had been drugged. Gerry didn't know whether to laugh or cry; her boss was smiling idiotically, singing softly to herself.

Then Tom was there, holding her as if he would never let go, tears streaming down his face. It took Gerry a few moments to realise that her own cheeks were wet.

'I'd say that was the perfect take-down, wouldn't you?' Tony had appeared at Gerry's side, and was watching appreciatively as Comfrey was led away.

'Yeah,' Gerry said. 'Sometimes it goes just right. Thank goodness it happened that way tonight.'

'What on earth has he given her?' Tom said anxiously. 'I can't stop her singing!'

'I'd say a hefty dose of a hallucinogen — acid or something,' said Colin, who had materialised out of nowhere. 'What is she singing?'

'Something about flowers in the rain, and how she wants to go on a submarine.'

'A yellow one, by any chance?' Colin laughed. 'She's back in the sixties — it's probably all those old pop records. Don't worry, it'll wear off, but she should be checked out in hospital. An ambulance is on its way.'

'So, that's it then,' said Tony.

'Killer and kidnapper,' added Luke. 'Two cases sorted in one arrest. That's a first, I must say.'

It was indeed, but one question remained. Why had Comfrey killed the people responsible for Amelia's death? What connection could he possibly have to the Sixty-four Club? Right now, Gerry was too tired to even guess at an answer. It was enough to have Kate back with them, without a shot having been fired. Tomorrow was another day.

EPILOGUE

It was two months before Kate, accompanied by Gerry, went back to Knighton House, this time to thank Barney, along with Arthur and Lottie Montgomery. Without their help, who knew what Jude Comfrey would have done with her.

It had been a strange couple of months. Months in which she was subject to a roller-coaster of emotions. But with the help and encouragement of Tom, along with Julia Tennant, she was now back on track. Many questions remained unanswered, mainly because Jude Comfrey would not speak. When, after a month, he still hadn't uttered a word, Kate realised she would have to look elsewhere. But this, too, was impossible, since her only other source of information was even more silent. The inquest on Enid Houghton had returned an open verdict. Both Kate and Gerry were certain that the mystery resident who had visited Enid just before her collapse was Jude Comfrey. It tied in with his absence, and what he'd told her about something he had to do. But there was no proof. He could just as well have gone into the hidden passages to switch on the lamps, ready for their escape. And Jude was saying nothing.

Kate parked her car outside the old house but didn't get out immediately.

'Does it bring back bad memories?' asked Gerry.

'No, not exactly. I don't really have that many memories. Those bloody drugs he gave me — half the time I was tripping.' She looked sideways at Gerry. 'You're absolutely certain no one took a sneaky video of me after my rescue? It's just that I've been told I was belting out sixties pop songs.'

Gerry grinned at her. 'It's all right; you won't be going viral on TikTok.'

'I guess it wasn't my finest hour.'

'Come on, don't be so modest. Just think, how many people could have managed to get a smartwatch out of a trouser pocket while being trussed up like a turkey, and then send their location? I think it was very impressive.'

Kate smiled. 'The tricky bit was not dropping it. With my hands tied together, I had to ease it out of my pocket, balance it on my knees and set it to share my location with you. Then I had to get it back again before he returned.'

They sat looking up at the house until Gerry roused herself. 'Come on, let's go and see our friends. I'm concerned about what's going to happen to them now that Enid is dead. I suppose they'll all have to look for somewhere else to live, and it certainly won't be anything like this.'

'Just as well,' said Kate. 'I'd rather live in a tent than this place.'

'With three kids and a small menagerie? I'd like to see that!'

The two of them got out of the car and made for the newly mended front door. As they drew near, it opened, and Barney Capstick appeared, looking surprisingly cheerful.

He beamed at them. 'Come in, come in. Arthur and Lottie are expecting you. Lottie's even made a cake. We're having a little celebration.'

Inside the flat, she thanked them for what they'd done for her. In recognition of their outstanding contribution to the forces of law and order, the superintendent was inviting them to the station the following week to convey his thanks. 'The local rag will be covering it, and there'll be refreshments.'

Barney grinned at the Montgomerys. 'Things are really going our way, aren't they?'

'Come and have tea,' Lottie said, 'and we'll tell you all about it.'

Over tea, and slices of delicious chocolate cake, Arthur gave them the news.

'Of course, it will take a while for it to come to fruition,' he began. 'But, well, a few days ago we received a letter from Enid's solicitor. It seems that, in the absence of any living relatives, she has left Knighton House along with the estate to Lottie and me.'

'Wow!' Gerry exclaimed. 'That's amazing.'

Kate wondered if that was quite as wonderful as it seemed. The place was a money pit, and everyone said that Enid had been on her uppers. How on earth would they cope?

Arthur had evidently noticed her dubious expression. 'I know what you're thinking, DI Carter, but it turns out that Enid's financial situation wasn't as dire as she liked to make out. In fact, it was completely different. Despite what she said, she did have money. She simply stopped spending on the house after that dreadful Eric Payne — or whatever his real name is — started blackmailing her.'

'We don't actually know that, dear,' said Lottie. 'But she was paying him large sums of money. The solicitor suspects that he knew something about her, or possibly her daughter or granddaughter, and that she was paying him to remain silent.'

'But there is money left, enough to keep things afloat until . . .' Arthur paused dramatically. 'And this is the best bit! There was an offer on the table, which Enid refused at the time, but it still stands.'

'A large company wants to purchase Knighton House and convert it into luxury accommodation for the over-sixties. The gardens are to be managed by a permanent gardener-groundsman—'

They all looked at Barney, who grinned broadly. 'Who will have his own cottage on site.'

'As soon as the will is finalised, we will start negotiations,' said Arthur. 'The offer is a very generous one; we would be fools not to accept it, especially as it allows us to remain here, rent-free. We just need to ensure Enid's special requirements for the garden are upheld.'

'And what are they?' asked Kate.

'Simply that the family burial ground shall remain a private place, properly cared for,' Lottie explained. 'She wished to ensure that Amelia has fresh flowers every week, and her grave is tended and kept neat. She'd be so pleased to know Barney will be the one to do it.'

'And Enid? I know her body has yet to be released for burial, but is she to come here too?' Kate asked.

'Yes,' Arthur said, suddenly serious. 'Although she is to be cremated, if the coroner permits. She has left a letter containing her wishes concerning the disposal of her remains. She wants no grave marker, no headstone. Her ashes are to be buried in a far corner of the grounds and left untouched. She wants no one to know she is there.'

'Poor Enid,' said Lottie sadly. 'She was a very religious woman, you know. We think she believed that in taking her own life, she committed a mortal sin and so did not deserve to be buried with her family in consecrated ground.'

'I know what they say,' Arthur added, 'but we are certain that she committed suicide. After Amelia died, she had nothing left to live for, and doubly so when that man started draining her remaining resources. She put her house in order, so to speak, only three weeks before she died.'

Kate nodded. It was a perfectly understandable conclusion to come to, and she could only be delighted that things had turned out well for them. Barney, too, had a well-deserved new life with a regular job and a secure home. No wonder he couldn't stop smiling.

Kate and Gerry got up to leave, saying they would see the three of them at the station next week.

Back in the car, they sat for a while in silence.

Finally, Kate said, 'They got it wrong, didn't they?'

'They got one thing right though,' said Gerry. 'Enid Houghton was not the woman she pretended to be.'

Kate gave a bitter laugh. 'You're right there. One thing we do know about Comfrey was that he was a hired killer, he told me so himself. We also know that he had no connection whatsoever to Amelia or the Sixty-four Club. Enid did.'

'Those large payments were a business transaction, weren't they, not blackmail at all. Enid Houghton was eaten up with hate for the people who caused her granddaughter's death. She was righting a terrible wrong, in the only way she knew how.' Gerry let out a long breath. 'But if Comfrey remains silent, we'll never get enough evidence for the Crown Prosecution Service.'

Kate shrugged. That was true. Believing something was one thing, proving it was another.

'I do wonder how Enid knew how to get in contact with a hitman,' said Gerry. 'Most people wouldn't have a clue where to start.'

The thought had crossed Kate's mind too, but the investigation into Jude Comfrey was showing that he constantly moved around the country, renting somewhere to stay until his current job was completed, then moving on. Most likely he had moved into Knighton House after he had killed the man in the hit-and-run incident he professed to have witnessed. He had seen her and his obsession began. He moved to Knighton House to be close to her.

Gerry agreed with her assessment. 'I remember Arthur telling me that Enid was an excellent judge of character. So, maybe she saw it in him, saw what he was, or our chatty Arthur could have mentioned the granddaughter's death and how it had affected the old lady, and Comfrey planted the idea in her mind.'

'We'll probably never know the truth,' Kate said. 'Julia Tennant reckons Jude Comfrey will never talk. His obsession with me was so all-consuming that losing me has rendered his life meaningless.'

Gerry shuddered. 'Scary bloody creep! At least they found the knife he used to murder those people in his belongings, and Colin has confirmed that it was the murder weapon. Comfrey will go down for life.'

Kate's face lit up at the mention of Colin. 'Now there's another good outcome. Cold Colin is moving in with his Uncle Fergus so he can look after him, and don't you dare tell anyone, but he's seeing Julia Tennant for therapy. I bumped into him at her consulting room in Cartoft. He said there had been a family tragedy that he had never come to terms with, but was, thanks to Julia, beginning to let it go. Cold Colin isn't cold anymore.'

Gerry grinned. 'Thank heavens for that! We've all come out of it well, haven't we? You are back with your family, and as for me, Nathan and I have finally got a settlement from my husband and are about to move into a nice little flat in town. I might even say that everything is coming up roses!'

Kate smiled. It was . . . but as she started the engine and drove away from Knighton House, she realised there was one thing that would always haunt her. Somewhere, not too far away, locked behind prison walls, was an insane man with a burning obsession . . . for her. What if he found a way to . . . ?

THE END

THE JOFFE BOOKS STORY

We began in 2014 when Jasper agreed to publish his mum's much-rejected romance novel and it became a bestseller.

Since then we've grown into the largest independent publisher in the UK. We're extremely proud to publish some of the very best writers in the world, including Joy Ellis, Faith Martin, Caro Ramsay, Helen Forrester, Simon Brett and Robert Goddard. Everyone at Joffe Books loves reading and we never forget that it all begins with the magic of an author telling a story.

We are proud to publish talented first-time authors, as well as established writers whose books we love introducing to a new generation of readers.

We won Trade Publisher of the Year at the Independent Publishing Awards in 2023 and Best Publisher Award in 2024 at the People's Book Prize. We have been shortlisted for Independent Publisher of the Year at the British Book Awards for the last five years, and were shortlisted for the Diversity and Inclusivity Award at the 2022 Independent Publishing Awards. In 2023 we were shortlisted for Publisher of the Year at the RNA Industry Awards, and in 2024 we were shortlisted at the CWA Daggers for the Best Crime and Mystery Publisher.

We built this company with your help, and we love to hear from you, so please email us about absolutely anything bookish at feedback@joffebooks.com.

If you want to receive free books every Friday and hear about all our new releases, join our mailing list here: www.joffebooks.com/freebooks.

And when you tell your friends about us, just remember: it's pronounced Joffe as in coffee or toffee!